The Mystery of the
MISSING
DINOSAURS

CAROLE MARSH
MYSTERIES™

by
Carole Marsh

Published by Gallopade International/Carole Marsh Books. Printed in the United States of America.

Editorial Assistant: Michael Longmeyer

Cover design: Steve St. Laurent; Editor: Jenny Corsey; Graphic Design: Steve St. Laurent; Layout and footer design: Lynette Rowe; Photography: Amanda McCutcheon.

Also available:
The Mystery of the Missing Dinosaurs Teacher's Guide

Gallopade is proud to be a member and supporter of these educational organizations and associations:

American Booksellers Association
American Library Association
International Reading Association
National Association for Gifted Children
The National School Supply and Equipment Association
The National Council for the Social Studies
Museum Store Association
Association of Partners for Public Lands

What Kids Say About Carole Marsh Mysteries . . .

I love the real locations! Reading the book always makes me want to go and visit them all on our next family vacation. My Mom says maybe, but I can't wait!

One day, I want to be a real kid in one of Ms. Marsh's mystery books. I think it would be fun, and I think I am a real character anyway. I filled out the application and sent it in and am keeping my fingers crossed!

History was not my favorite subject till I starting reading Carole Marsh Mysteries. Ms. Marsh really brings history to life. Also, she leaves room for the scary and fun.

I think Christina is so smart and brave. She is lucky to be in the mystery books because she gets to go to a lot of places. I always wonder just how much of the book is true and what is made up. Trying to figure that out is fun!

Grant is cool and funny! He makes me laugh a lot!!

I like that there are boys and girls in the story of different ages. Some mysteries I outgrow, but I can always find a favorite character to identify with in these books.

They are scary, but not too scary. They are funny. I learn a lot.
There is always food which makes me hungry. I feel like I am there.

What Adults Say About Carole Marsh Mysteries . . .

*I think kids love these books because they have such a wealth of detail.
I know I learn a lot reading them! It's an engaging way to look at the
history of any place or event. I always say I'm only going to read one
chapter to the kids, but that never happens—it's always two or three, at
least! —Librarian*

*Reading the mystery and going on the field trip—Scavenger Hunt in
hand—was the most fun our class ever had! It really brought the place
and its history to life. They loved the real kids characters and all the
humor. I loved seeing them learn that reading is an experience to
enjoy! —4th grade teacher*

*Carole Marsh is really on to something with these unique mysteries.
They are so clever; kids want to read them all. The Teacher's Guides
are chock full of activities, recipes, and additional fascinating
information. My kids thought I was an expert on the subject—and
with this tool, I felt like it! —3rd grade teacher*

*My students loved writing their own Real Kids/Real Places mystery
book! Ms. Marsh's reproducible guidelines are a real jewel. They
learned about copyright and more & ended up with their own book
they were so proud of! —Reading/Writing Teacher*

This book is dedicated to Avery,
my newest granddaughter and future mystery book heroine.

This book is a complete work of fiction. All events are
fictionalized, and although the first names of real children
are used, their characterization in this book is fiction.

For additional information on Carole Marsh Mysteries, visit:
www.carolemarshmysteries.com

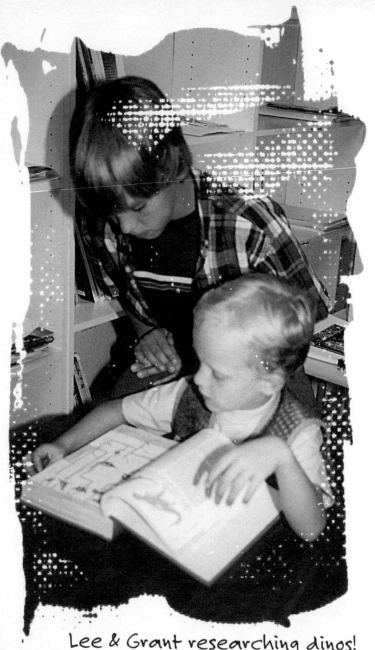

Lee & Grant researching dinos!

20 YEARS AGO...

As a mother and an author, one of the fondest periods of my life was when I decided to write mystery books for children. At this time (1979) kids were pretty much glued to the TV, something parents and teachers complained about the way they do about video games today.

I decided to set each mystery in a real place—a place kids could go and visit for themselves after reading the book. And I also used real children as characters. Usually a couple of my own children served as characters, and I had no trouble recruiting kids from the book's location to also be characters.

Also, I wanted all the kids—boys and girls of all ages—to participate in solving the mystery. And, I wanted kids to learn something as they read. Something about the history of the location. And I wanted the stories to be funny.

That formula of real+scary+smart+fun served me well. The kids and I had a great time visiting each site and many of the events in the stories actually came out of our experiences there. (For example, we really did ride the Ferris wheel at the Navy Pier and look out over the city from the top of the Sears Tower!)

I love getting letters from teachers and parents who say they read the book with their class or child, then visited the historic site and saw all the places in the mystery for themselves. What's so great about that? What's great is that you and your children have an experience that bonds you together forever. Something you shared. Something you both cared about at the time. Something that crossed all age levels—a good story, a good scare, a good laugh!

20 years later,

Carole Marsh

**Christina
Yother**

**Grant
Yother**

**Alex
Brilliant**

**Lana
Gillen**

ABOUT THE CHARACTERS

Christina Yother, 9, from Peachtree City, Georgia

Grant Yother, 7, from Peachtree City, Georgia
Christina's brother

Alex Brilliant as Lee Coyle, 11, from Chicago, Illinois

Lana Gillen, as Lana, Lee's sister, 10, from Chicago,
 Illinois is the daughter of a Gallopade International
 sales associate.

The many places featured in the book actually exist and are
worth a visit! Perhaps you could read the book and see some of
the places the kids visited during their mysterious adventure!

TITLES IN THE CAROLE MARSH MYSTERIES SERIES

Books and Teacher's Guides are available at booksellers, libraries, school supply stores, museums, and many other locations!

CONTENTS

1 BEACH DREAMS

"One plus two plus eight plus one equals twelve," Grant said aloud to himself. It was the last day of first grade, and Grant was counting the hours until he hit the ocean waves with his brand new boogie board. He was pretty good at math even though it was not his favorite subject, but he decided to count the hours up one more time just to be sure. *One* hour until the bell rings, *two* hours until the car is loaded and his family gets on the road, *eight* hours to drive to Florida to their hotel, and *one* hour (or less!) to unpack the car, and for his Dad to take him out to the beach! "Yep, that's twelve!" Grant told himself.

Grant had been anxiously waiting all year for this trip. For Christmas, he had gotten a brand new boogie board from Mimi and Papa, his grandparents, and he couldn't wait to get out in the water and ride the waves with

Last Day Of School!

Last Day Of School

1

it. It was dark blue with lightning bolts down the sides and sure to be the coolest board on the beach.

BRRRIIINNNGGG! The bell blared and startled Grant out of his daydreams. "Down to eleven hours now," he said.

"What's eleven?" his friend Wingho asked.

"Eleven hours until I'm shredding some waves on my board," Grant told him.

"Well, have fun and call me when you get back so I can beat you again in soccer," Wingho said with a laugh.

"Ohhh-kay," Grant yelled over his shoulder, as he ran out the door to catch his bus home. He zigzagged all the way to the bus, yelling goodbyes to all the friends and teachers that he passed. As he climbed the steps to the bus, he saw a familiar face in the very front seat.

"Grant, sit here!" his sister yelled. Christina was as excited as Grant about this beach trip. Even though she was not into boogie boarding, she did love swimming in the waves and she especially loved all the great seafood that they got to eat at the beach!

"Eleven hours," Grant said in a matter-of-fact tone to Christina.

"Eleven what?" she asked.

"In eleven hours, yours truly will be hitting the

Last Day Of
School

School's Out!

beach and using my new boogie board," he told her smugly.

"Actually, you won't," she informed him even more smugly. "Because in eleven hours it will be two o'clock in the morning, and I don't think Mom and Dad are gonna let you swim in the dark."

"Aw, shucks," Grant moaned. "It will be harder to sleep tonight than on Christmas Eve. I hope Dad is ready to get up early, because I want to be the first one on the beach in the morning."

Grant spent the rest of the ride pouting over his math miscalculations, while Christina chatted with her friends about hanging out at the pool for the rest of the summer once she got back from the beach.

"Get off, slowpoke!" Christina said, as she elbowed Grant out of the seat. "We're home."

They both rushed off the bus, waving goodbyes to their friends and the driver, and raced down the driveway. The anticipation of leaving for the beach had them both so excited that Grant didn't even care that Christina beat him to the door. He just wanted to grab his suitcase and boogie board and help Dad pack the car so they could hurry up and leave.

As they both plowed though the doorway they were quite surprised to find Mom sitting on the couch with tears

School's Out!

We're Home!

in her eyes. Dad had wrapped his arm around her, trying to comfort her.

"Hey, Mom. Hey, Dad," Christina said, as she dropped her book bag and ran into the living room. "What's wrong? Why aren't you packing the car?"

"It's only eleven hours plus one night's sleep until I hit the beach," Grant reminded them.

"Well, kids," Dad said slowly. "I have some bad news. We aren't going to Florida anymore. We have to cancel the trip."

"What? You can't be serious!" Christina shouted, not sure whether to be angry or start crying.

"Why can't we go?" Grant asked, hoping it must be a joke his Dad was playing on him.

"Kids, I know how much you were looking forward to this vacation, but now we have to go to Chicago," their father told them.

Grant and Christina still didn't understand. Chicago? Why? They looked at their mother for an explanation.

"I have some really bad news," their mother said between sobs. "Your Uncle Michael has been kidnapped!"

What's Wrong?   No Beach Vacation

2 MISSING BONES, MISSING UNCLE

"Uncle Michael. . . kidnapped?!" Christina exclaimed.

"Wha-wha-what happened?" stammered Grant, as he dropped down to sit on the floor. He couldn't believe that something had happened to his uncle. Uncle Michael always sent them the coolest gifts. He was a paleontologist who spent a lot of time looking for dinosaur fossils out in New Mexico and Arizona. To Grant it seemed like the best job in the world. Once his uncle had sent him a shark's tooth bigger than Grant's own hand! He had taken it for show-and-tell at school, and it had been the biggest hit of the year.

Dad explained the situation. "As you know, your uncle finds dinosaur bones for the Field Museum in Chicago. Well, a few months ago, he found a new one and

No Beach
Vacation

Kidnapped?

spent the last three months digging it up and getting it ready to take to the museum. He was personally driving the truck, where the bones were stored, to the museum in Chicago and was supposed to be there two nights ago. The last time your Aunt Cassidy talked to him, he had stopped in St. Louis for gas and food. He didn't get home that night or the next. So she called the museum. They told her that the truck was parked in back of the building and your Uncle Michael's jacket was in the truck, but neither he nor the dinosaur were anywhere to be found."

"So we gotta go find him! And the dinosaur!" Grant shouted. He and Christina had been involved in a number of mystery adventures. Their Mimi and Papa always seemed to be dragging them off on an adventure somewhere. Of course, Mimi was a mystery writer, so it was only fit that she would get caught up in some mysteries of her own.

"No, kids!" Mom told them in a stern voice. "You're not going to gallivant all through the streets of Chicago. Your Mimi and Papa may let you run all around on your own solving mysteries and getting into danger, but Mom and Dad are going with you this time, and you are staying in my sight at all times! We are just going to visit and comfort your Aunt Cassidy and Cousin Avery. The *police* are the

Kidnapped?

No Solving Mysteries!

ones who will handle *this* mystery."

"But Mom, Uncle Michael needs our help!" Christina pleaded to her mother.

"The police will handle it. Now you two go upstairs and unpack your beach stuff from your suitcases and get ready for the trip to Chicago. We're leaving on Papa's plane in three hours." Dad instructed them, pointing upstairs.

The kids stomped their feet the whole way down the hall and upstairs to their rooms. Christina mumbled to herself that she could figure out where her Uncle Michael was, if they would just let her.

Grant just ran straight to his suitcase and dumped everything out on the bed. Then he started cramming shorts, t-shirts, socks, and underwear back into it. When he picked up his bathing suit, he looked at it sadly and carefully set it aside in hopes that he would still get to use it soon.

As Grant headed back downstairs, he grabbed his "dinosaur vest" from the closet and put it on. His vest was a birthday present from Mimi. It was his favorite thing to wear. It had pockets everywhere, which he had stuffed to the max with dinosaur toys, a magnifying glass, flashlight, compass, and all the other little things that he never knew if and when he might need.

No Solving Mysteries!

Repack Suitcases

Grant tugged his suitcase down the stairs, one loud CLOMP at a time. He was just a few steps behind Christina, who was also carrying her neatly packed bag downstairs to the front door. They both dragged their bags straight to the car where Dad put them in the trunk. Then the foursome headed off to the airport.

No one was happy.

Repack
Suitcases

To The
Airport

3 TAKEOFF!

As Dad drove them to the airport, Christina pulled out the cell phone that Mom had given her to carry in case there was ever an emergency. Not that she was planning on calling anyone. She had already discovered that it was only for real emergencies, not like the time when she called to find out what her best friend was wearing to school the next day. That mistake had gotten her grounded for two weeks!

The coolest thing about the phone was that she could send e-mails with it. And that, she *was* allowed to do. She slowly spelled out a message to her best friend, Emily, who she had hoped to meet up with at the beach:

To The Airport

Sending A Message

NO BEACH, GONE
TO CHICAGO.

About that time the car stopped, and everyone piled out. This was not the busy airport that they usually flew out of. Usually there were crowds of people, pilots, security guards, and luggage, but not today. All Christina could see was one small plane that Papa was walking around, kicking on the tires. Papa had spent the last six months taking flying lessons and only needed a few more practice flights to receive his flight license.

"Ok, kids," Dad told them. "Get your suitcase and take it to Papa's plane."

"Mimi and Papa are going, too!" shouted Christina excitedly. This trip might not be so bad after all, she thought to herself.

Sending A
Message

Papa's Plane!

"Papa, Papa, Papa," Grant yelled, as he tugged his suitcase as fast as he could towards the plane. "Can I sit up front with you and help fly the plane?"

"Sure Grant, you can fly the plane and I'll take a nap until we get there. How about that?" Papa joked.

"But Papa," Grant replied, a little worried, "I've never *really* flown a plane."

"Well, you're never too young to learn, that's what I say. Just look at me. You can sit up in the front between the pilot and me. I'll give you your first flying lesson on our way to Chicago," Papa told him.

Once the bags were loaded, Mimi made Papa take a third walk around the little plane to be sure everything was OK. Then they all buckled in and got ready for takeoff. The pilot radioed the control tower and was informed to be ready for takeoff in five minutes.

"Ladies and gentlemen," Papa began in his really deep voice over a pretend pretzel microphone, "This is your co-pilot Papa speaking. Please buckle up and prepare for takeoff. We'll be leaving in five minutes for the Windy City. Your flight attendant today is Mimi, and she will be providing her famous snickerdoodle cookies and pink lemonade once we are in the air."

"Be sure to turn off your cell phones," Mimi

Papa's Plane!

Ready for Takeoff

reminded everyone. "You're not supposed to leave them on while the plane is in the air."

When Christina pulled hers out to turn it off, an idea hit her. She typed a quick message to her Uncle Michael and hit SEND. Then she hit the OFF button and stuck the phone inside her little pink purse. Papa revved up the engines, and the plane was airborne in no time. Christina leaned back in her seat and settled in for the long flight and a nap. And to wonder where in the world her Uncle Michael could be.

Ready for
Takeoff

Where's Uncle
Michael?

4 TRAPPED IN THE DARK

BLINK... BLINK... SQUINT. It was so dark where he was, that no matter how hard he tried, he couldn't see a thing. He was lying on a hard floor. There was a dull ache in his back and his head was throbbing, but what had really awakened him was the thing that pulsed and dug hard into his hip.

"Ouch!" he moaned, as he rolled onto his back. He put his hand to his head and could feel some dried blood right where the pounding headache was strongest. The room smelled like a fireplace. He coughed from the soot that seemed to be stuck in his dry throat.

He had no idea where he was, or how he had gotten here. The last thing Uncle Michael could remember was pulling the truck into the garage in

Where Am I?

How Did I Get Here?

back of the Field Museum. It had been 4:00 a.m., so he had just locked up the truck and the garage and was walking out to his car. He remembered that it was parked right next to a black van. He had walked out to his car and was trying to get his key in the lock when he felt a sharp pain to the back of his head. Then everything went black.

Now he was lying in a dark room, on a hard floor, and had no idea what was happening. After a quick check, he realized that his wallet, his jacket, and his cell phone were gone. He got up and felt around the walls. He found a door handle and twisted it, but it was locked. He banged on the door and yelled for help. Nothing.

What's going on here? he asked himself. Panic started to overcome him, as he realized that he was trapped in this room. Who knows where? he thought. And he had no idea who had put him here, or why!

"What is that sticking into my hip?" He felt for the painful lump and found a small box stuck on his belt.

"My pager!" Uncle Michael realized excitedly. Whoever had taken his phone and wallet must not have realized that this was left hooked on the side of

How Did I Get Here?

What's Going On?

his belt.

When he pushed the button, the small screen lit up. It wasn't very bright, but he held it up enough for him to look around the room. The room was totally bare. Just concrete walls and a single door that he already knew was locked.

He pulled the pager back down and looked at the screen to see why it kept vibrating. There were 15 messages from his wife, Cassidy. Judging by the message times, it looked like it had been two days since he had parked the truck and walked to his car. She must be very worried about him. He read through each message from his wife, asking him to call her. Then his eyes jumped to the last message on the screen. It read simply,

WHERE R U?
TIA.

His heart raced as he realized what this meant. It was from his niece, Christina. She knew he was missing, and so surely the police must be out looking for him. He bet that Christina and Grant and the

What's Going On?

I Have My Pager!

rest of the gang were headed to Chicago. If only he could figure out where he was and send a message to Christina!

He looked at the screen one last time. When he started to type in his reply, his heart sunk as he realized that he couldn't send letters from his pager, only numbers. Dejectedly, he lay back on the floor. He wanted to cry. But then he decided to type the one thing that kept going though his mind.

Uncle Michael pressed the numbers on his pager slowly–then pushed the SEND button. He put his arms behind his head, shut his eyes, and waited.

I Have My Pager!

Only Numbers

5 WENDY WHO?

"So why do they call her Wendy?" Grant asked Papa.

"Who?" Papa asked back, confused.

"You said we are going to the Wendy City, so I was wondering why Chicago is called Wendy," Grant explained to his grandfather.

"Ha, ha, ha," Papa chuckled. "Not Wendy, but Wi-i-indy. Like the wind that blows in the trees." Papa took a deep breath, turned towards Grant, and blew at his hair. "*Windy!*"

"Some say they call it the 'Windy City' because of the winds that blow off of Lake Michigan," Mimi explained to Grant and everyone else in the plane. "Others call it the Windy City because they say the politicians are so full of hot air!"

"Chicago is also full of really cool museums," Mimi

Wendy?

Oh, Windy!

added. "Papa and I have been here at least ten times just to visit different museums. Of course, our favorite is the Field Museum of Natural History where Sue is."

"Who Sue, Sue who?" Christina asked, waking up from her nap. She realized she was missing out on the cookies, as she looked over and saw Grant with one in each hand with a bite out of both.

"Sue," Mimi explained, "is the name of the Tyrannosaurus Rex dinosaur that your Uncle Michael helped dig up a few years ago. They have it displayed in the museum, and it is spectacular!"

"Rrrrggghhhhh!!" Grant yelled. "I'm not scared of a T-Rex, especially one named Sue! One day I'm going to find the biggest, meanest, scariest dinosaur of them all. I will call it the Grantosaurus!"

"You should call it the Squirtosaurus," Christina joked.

"Mom! Dad!" Grant hollered, "Make her say she's sorry!"

"Kids, settle down," Dad told them. "Papa needs to concentrate while he helps fly the plane. One day he'll be flying us around all by himself."

Hearing his name, Papa turned around and said, "My favorite thing about Chicago is all the delicious food!

Oh, Windy!

Delicious food!

Speaking of food, Mimi, how about passing out some more of those delicious snickerdoodle cookies you made."

"Ummm, they're almost gone, Papa," Grant mumbled between bites of his fourth cookie as Mimi grabbed the last two off the plate. She stuck one in Papa's open mouth. He mumbled, "Thnkks!"

"Grant, you sure eat like a T-Rex," his mother told him, as she wiped the crumbs off his face with a napkin.

"I'm *saury*," said Grant, flashing a big grin before he laid back in his seat for a quick nap.

Delicious food!

Mmmm . . . Cookies!

6 MY KINDA TOWN

The tall skyscrapers of Chicago slowly came into view on the horizon. The city, nestled on the banks of Lake Michigan, was a beautiful sight from the air. Papa gracefully steered the plane in the direction of the impressive skyline.

Christina and Grant both slept through the pilot and Papa's smooth landing and were still half asleep as their mother guided them off the plane and towards the car. The next thing they remembered was the car stopping again and everyone unloading the suitcases and telling them to come on.

"Don't you want to see your Aunt Cassidy and your Cousin Avery?" Mimi asked.

"Aunt Cassidy!" Christina exclaimed, running up the stairs and ringing the doorbell over and over.

Landing In
Chicago!

Aunt Cassidy's
House

She was quite startled when a man she had never met opened the door and looked at her sternly. "Can I help you?" he asked.

"Uhh, is my Aunt Cassidy here?" she replied. About that time, she saw Aunt Cassidy come around the corner. Christina scooted by the strange man and ran to give her aunt a big hug.

The rest of the family hurried in the house and hugs were given all around as Mimi headed straight for the baby. Avery was only three months old, and was so much bigger than the last time Mimi had held her, soon after she was born.

"Cas," Papa began, "We're so sorry about Michael. Don't you worry, the police will figure out what is going on. I'm sure that everything is OK."

"I'm so glad that you all came. I'm trying to be strong, but it's just hard because I'm so worried," Aunt Cassidy said. She dabbed at her eyes with a tissue.

Grant had been keeping an eye on the strange man. When he just couldn't wait any longer, he blurted out, "Who is *he*?"

The man stepped forward and shook hands with the adults. He told them, "I'm Marcus Coyle. I'm Uncle Michael's partner. We hunt for dinosaur bones together.

Aunt Cassidy's House

Who Are You?

Who are you?

He and I met when we were helping to dig up Sue a few years ago. After that we decided to team up and search together for new fossils."

The man sat down and continued. "About six months ago, we found a T-Rex almost identical to Sue–with one problem. There was no skull attached to the bones. But since the body was so perfect, we decided to dig it up for the museum," Marcus said. "We nicknamed him Louis, after King Louis XVI of France, who was beheaded. We still haven't solved the mystery of why the dinosaur is missing his head. But that's one of the reasons that the police are so suspicious, considering what happened at the museum the same night your Uncle Michael disappeared."

"What do you mean?" Mimi asked him anxiously.

"Well, that same night," Marcus said, "someone broke into the Field Museum and stole Sue's head right out of the exhibit! The police think that Uncle Michael is involved in a conspiracy. He has a key to the museum, and he was there that night. Also, he just happens to be the only person to have the only other fully-intact T-Rex body in the world," Marcus finished.

Then he added, "A T-Rex in need of a head."

"Well, I know my uncle didn't do it!" Christina said angrily. "You can tell the police that he needs help, not to

get arrested."

"We all know that Uncle Michael wouldn't steal anything. But the police just think it's all too suspicious," Aunt Cassidy explained to them. "Once Uncle Michael is found and the bones are recovered, then everything will be OK. Marcus has been going through his files looking for any clues as to who might have done this."

"Well, you let us know if you need any help," Papa said. "In the meantime, I think we all need to get something to eat. Who's hungry?"

"I'm hungry as a T-Rex!" Grant shouted.

"C'mon then, Sue. Let's go unpack so we can go eat," Christina teased him.

"Mommm!" Grant fussed, "She's teasing me again."

"I'm *saury!*" Christina laughed, as she ran off to put her suitcase in the spare room where she would be sleeping.

Towering
T-Rex

Missing
T-Rex

7 GET A CLUE!

They all piled into Aunt Cassidy's minivan so Papa could drive them to the restaurant. Christina noticed the matching license plates on the minivan and Uncle Michael's car, parked next to it. The two license plates said *Mr. Bones* and *Mrs. Bones*. Uncle Michael sure loves his dinosaurs, she thought to herself.

"Tonight we go to the Berghoff, where you can get delicious sauerbraten or wienerschnitzel," Papa told them.

"Burp Off? Sour What? Wiener Who?" Grant asked, puzzled.

"It's German food and it's delicious. It's all stuff that every Meatosaurus would devour. I'm sure a T-Grant will love it, too!" Mimi kidded.

During the drive, Christina played with baby Avery in her car seat. She was thinking to herself what

Into The
Minivan

Off To The
Berghoff

possibilities there could be to explain the disappearance of her Uncle Michael. She knew that he couldn't have stolen those dinosaurs. You don't just walk around town with a T-Rex head hanging over your shoulder! It was going to be up to her to solve this mystery.

Just then a cell phone rang, and Aunt Cassidy answered it quickly. "Hello?" she asked quietly. After a long pause she said, "Ok, Marcus, we'll see you and your kids at the Berghoff in ten minutes. Bye."

After she hung up her phone, she told the rest of the family that they would have company for dinner. Marcus, his wife, and their two kids, Lee, 11, and Lana, 10, would be joining them at the restaurant.

Grant was excited. It was nice to hang out with older boys. They always knew so much cool stuff. He hoped that Lee liked dinosaurs as much as he did.

The sound of the phone reminded Christina that she hadn't checked her phone for e-mails from Emily yet. She grabbed her phone out of her purse, turned it on, and hit the CHECK button. The phone blinked and beeped twice. Christina was excited because she knew that meant she had a message.

She wondered what Emily was going to say about her sudden change of plans. Surprised, she realized that

Off To The
Berghoff

A Phone
Message

the message wasn't from her friend–it was from Uncle Michael!

That was all it said. Christina thought to herself, he's in trouble! Why didn't he just send her a message telling them where he was? Who would she tell? The police would not believe that this meant he wasn't guilty of stealing the dinosaurs. She couldn't tell her Mom or Dad. They would tell the police and then take her phone away. Maybe . . . Papa? No. She would just keep this to herself for now.

I need a clue, she thought to herself. Christina quickly punched out another message. As Papa pulled the car to the front of the restaurant to drop them off, Grant crawled over her lap in a rush to get out of the car. She

A Phone
Message

Sending A
Message

finished her message and punched the SEND button. Then
she crossed her fingers–all of them!

Sending A
Message

Crossing Her
Fingers!

8 NEW FRIENDS ...
AND SOME
BRATS!

They were led to a huge table in the back. Grant and Christina were seated next to the other two kids who were already at the table.

"You must be Christina and Grant," the older boy said, as they sat down. "I'm Lee," he told them as he pointed his thumb at himself. "This is Lana, she's my little sis."

Christina looked over at Lee and then Lana. Not too little, she thought to herself. Lana was almost as tall as Lee.

"Hey, I'm Lana," she said, giving a quick wave to Grant and then Christina. "Don't listen to my 'big bro.' He's just teasing because I got better grades than he did on our final report cards."

"Wait till you get to the sixth grade and see how

Let's Eat!

Meet The Kids!

31

much homework you have; then we'll see who's laughing last," Lee argued back with his sister.

"Sooo," Grant butted in. "Where ya'll from?"

"We live here in Chicago," Lana answered him. "We used to live in Texas, California, and Virginia. We've moved a lot. Our Dad has worked for a lot of museums, but ever since he started working with the Field Museum, he just loves it. Hopefully we won't move anymore. I really like living in the Windy City."

"They don't call it windy because of the wind!" both Christina and Grant shouted at the same time.

Lana and Lee laughed and nodded their heads, "We know!"

While the adults carried on their conversations and Papa ordered appetizers and drinks, the kids continued learning details about each other. Christina decided that she really liked Lana a lot. If she lived in Peachtree City, she knew that the two of them would be good friends.

"So do you really think your Uncle Michael stole Sue and Louis?" Lee asked them finally.

"NO!" Grant yelled back. "He's no thief."

Christina leaned over the table and told them in a hushed voice, "I know he didn't do it and I can prove it. I sent him an e-mail with my cell phone, and this is the

Meet The Kids!

Look At This!

message he sent me back."

She pulled her phone out and showed each one of them the screen with the numbers 911 on it.

Grant's eyes widened. "That *really* came from Uncle Michael?" he asked.

"Yes, and that means he's in trouble and he needs our help. All we need is a clue, and since Lee and Lana live here, they can help us figure it out."

"Count me in," Lee told her quickly. "Ever since your uncle told us about the mysteries he helped solve when he was a kid, I have wanted something like this to happen."

"Well, we've already solved a few of our own, so we'll show you how it's done," Christina told the other kids proudly.

About that time, the waitress asked them what they would like to eat. When Lee said he wanted two "brats," Grant figured that sounded cool, so he ordered the same.

Christina just laughed and told him, "You are what you eat, brat!"

Look At This!

All We Need Is A Clue

9 BRATOSAURUS

During dinner, Grant learned that Lee seemed to know everything about dinosaurs. Lee told him about trips to the dino digs that he had made with his Dad. He even said that one time he had found his very own fossil. It turned out to be a small piece of a Stegosaurus leg. He had given the piece to the museum, but he also had a copy of it made to display in his bedroom.

"Look at this!" Grant told Lee, as he dug deep into the one of the pockets of his dinosaur vest. He pulled out a dark, heavy object and set it on the table with a dull thump.

"Wow, cool!" Lee said. "That's the biggest shark's tooth I've ever seen. It's even bigger than my hand!"

"My Uncle Michael found it, and he gave it to me," Grant said. "I don't want to go swimming in the water

Everything Dino!

Steg Leg & Shark Tooth

35

where this big Great White shark used to live!"

"So, what's on the shark's dinner menu tonight?" Lee joked with him. "Oh, yummy, it's Grantschnitzel." Both boys laughed and made up other funny words using each other's names, like "Lee-Rex!"

Across the table, Christina showed off her cell phone to Lana.

"That is so, cool! I can send an e-mail on my computer, and you can receive it on your phone?!" Lana asked.

"Yeah, and then I can send a message back to you on the computer. We can stay in touch even after we go back home to Georgia," Christina said.

The girls continued to talk phones and clothes and music and all other sorts of things that they seemed to have in common. Both groups of kids were oblivious to the conversations on the other end of the table among the adults.

"What would someone want to do with a dinosaur skeleton?" Christina and Grant's mother asked Marcus.

"Well, they are actually in very high demand," Marcus informed the adults. "Museums all want to have the newest, biggest, and best fossils uncovered. It's very competitive–sometimes outright cutthroat. When Sue was

Steg Leg &
Shark Tooth

Dino
Skeletons

discovered in South Dakota, museums from around the world fought over the rights to display her exhibit. There was even an attempted robbery on her bones while she was being dug up!" Marcus shook his head in disbelief.

"I was out there at the time helping with the dig," Marcus continued. "That's where I met Michael. In the middle of the night they caught some guys with a truck trying to steal the fossils that we had already dug up and put in crates to bring to Chicago. Apparently there is a big demand overseas on the black market for rare fossils."

Marcus shook his head and sighed. "That's why Michael was so paranoid about being involved in the delivery of Louis. He was afraid that something would happen to Louis before he could get him to the Field Museum here in Chicago."

"Looks like he was right," Cassidy said sadly.

"So why didn't you or some of the other archeologists help him drive it all the way back from New Mexico?" Papa asked Marcus.

"He wanted to do it by himself," Marcus responded. "He said we had all been away from home too long. He told us all to fly back ahead and spend some time with our families so we would be ready to unload and set up the fossils when he got here. Of course, the police think that

Dino Skeletons

Stealin' Bones

this was just an excuse for him to get the dinosaur alone so that he could steal it."

"Do *you* think he stole it?" Mimi asked slowly.

"No way," Marcus told her. "Michael is just like me. He wants to have dinosaurs on display for everyone to see, not hidden in some rich so-and-so's basement for only a few to enjoy. I think someone found out that he was driving back by himself and planned the robbery to occur at the same time so it would look like he was guilty. Probably whoever is involved needs him around to put the bones back together correctly."

"Hopefully the police will figure out this mystery before these crooks don't need Michael's help anymore," Papa said, causing Mimi to give him a strong elbow in the ribs.

"Just so that you know," Marcus continued. "Simon believes he is guilty and has hired a private investigator to track down Michael, Louis, and Sue's head."

"Who's Simon?" Mimi asked him.

Marcus began filling her in on the details. "Simon Donatello. He is our third partner. He doesn't do much of the fieldwork, but his family has the money that pays for our trips and equipment. He has spent over half a million dollars just for us to find and bring back Louis. The

Stealin'
Bones

A Third
Partner?

museum was going to give him $2 million for the bones. Would have been $3 million if we had found the skull, too."

"How much would something like that sell for on the black market?" Mimi asked.

"Geez, for the T-Rex body we just found, plus Sue's skull from the museum exhibit? I'd say a good $20 million," Marcus told her.

"Whheeeww!" Papa whistled. "I could buy a jet plane if I had that kind of money."

"You and your toys," Mimi kidded him. "Bigger boat, bigger car, bigger plane. Don't forget that's just more for us to keep clean, insured, and filled with gas!"

Right about then, Avery started crying.

"Somebody better get that baby a clean diaper!" Mimi said.

Suddenly, laughter exploded from the other end of the table. The adults could only make out a few words the kids were howling. "Dino . . . doodoo . . . Yuck!"

A Third
Partner?

Expensive
Bones

10 VILLAINOUS VISITORS

BUZZZZZ. BUZZZZZ. BUZZZZZ. Uncle Michael awoke suddenly, still sore, and still lying on the hard cement floor. The buzz of his pager meant one thing—another message! He sat up and reached over to pick up the pager. Uncle Michael hit a button to light up the screen. The light was not quite as bright as before. The battery showed that only a quarter of its power was left.

He popped the new message up on the screen:

```
WE R N CHICAGO.
NEED CLUE.  I'LL
FIND U.   TIA.
```

The thought that everyone knew he was missing lifted Uncle Michael's spirits a little. If his whole

Another Message!

They Know I Am Missing!

41

family had come all the way to Chicago, then the police must know he had been kidnapped. If only he could figure out what was going on, so he could send Christina a clue to give to the police.

He quickly turned off the pager to save the battery. In the pitch black darkness, Uncle Michael felt his way around the walls of the room. He reached the door and twisted the door handle with all his might. It wouldn't budge an inch. He started banging on the door and hollering for help. When his energy was gone and he had gotten no response, he crawled back to the center of the floor and laid down again.

Just then he heard a clicking noise, and the scraping of the door opening made him jerk up. The light that entered through the door was blinding. He hadn't seen light in three or four days, and it was burning his eyes. He saw a shadow in the doorway. It approached him and peered down with beady little eyes through a pair of wire-rimmed eyeglasses.

Uncle Michael recognized the man. He didn't know who he was, but he knew he had seen the man before. But more importantly, he remembered who he had seen the man with.

They Know I Am Missing!

I've Seen You Before

   The man threw down something at him that hit the floor with a thud. Uncle Michael reached over to pick it up and realized that it was a wrapped hamburger. He suddenly realized that he hadn't eaten in days. In only a few seconds, he consumed the entire burger. Faster than a T-Rex, he thought to himself, wondering how he could joke in such dire circumstances.

   The man then threw him a plastic bottle of water and spoke. "Drink up! It's all you get until tomorrow. You can bang on that door all you want, no one can hear you all the way down here."

   "Where am I?" Uncle Michael yelled at the man as he poured the refreshing liquid down his dry throat.

   "That's of no concern of yours, buddy. You better be glad you're still here and not on the bottom of Lake Michigan. But once we get the dinosaurs unpacked, we won't need you anymore," the rat-faced man told him.

   "What's going on? What are you doing with my dinosaurs?" Uncle Michael questioned the man.

   "OK, you might as well know . . . since you're, well, disposable. We have framed you for stealing

I've Seen
You Before

food!
Water!

Louis, breaking into the Field Museum, and stealing Sue's skull. We are selling them on the black market for $20 million. And you will take all the blame for it, while we get away with riches!" The man laughed and backed out of the doorway.

"You will never get away with this!" Uncle Michael screamed at him.

"We already have. We already have! And who would ever think to look for you right in the old basement of the museum. Ha ha!" The man continued laughing and slammed and locked the door leaving Uncle Michael alone in the dark.

But Uncle Michael was not sad. He had a big smile on his face. Now he knew where he was and who had kidnapped him and stolen Louis and Sue. The question he needed to answer was—how could he give this information to Christina?

In numbers. And, before his pager went dead! Dead. Uncle Michael didn't like thinking about that word.

I Know Where I Am Now!

The Clock Is Ticking

11 CONFUSING CLUES

Everyone headed out of the restaurant with full bellies. Christina followed Lana to her father's car and hopped in the backseat. Lee tagged along with Grant over to Aunt Cassidy's van where they climbed into the very back.

Christina leaned over and whispered secretively into Lana's ear. "My phone is buzzing. I'm getting another clue!"

Lana leaned back and they looked at each other, wide-eyed in anticipation, as Christina slowly reached into her purse to remove the phone. She clicked on the screen which read: You have 1 new message. While holding her breath, Christina slowly pressed the READ button. The message was simple:

Back To The Cars

Another Clue!

Between quick breaths Lana asked, "What does it mean? Is it a clue?"

"It must be a code, but I have no idea what it means. We *have* to figure it out. Uncle Michael's counting on us for help!" Christina told her emphatically.

"Maybe one of the boys will have an idea. Lee is really good with puzzles and codes. I will ask him when we get to the house," Lana said, trying to cheer up Christina.

Meanwhile, in the van, the boys were deep in a conversation of their own. Lee was telling Grant all about the famous mobsters who used to call Chicago home in the Roaring 1920s.

"Al Capone was their leader. He was the meanest gangster of all time," said Lee. "He called the people that

Another Clue!

Oh, No, In Code!

Is it a clue?

worked for him his henchmen. They had names like 'Needle-Nose' Nick, 'Terrible' Tony, and Joe 'Knuckles.'"

Grant thought for a few seconds and said, "Cool, I think I would call myself 'Greasy-finger' Grant, and you could be 'Look-out' Lee."

"Yeah and we could have tommyguns like all the gangsters used to carry," Lee chimed in.

"Tommy Gun?" Grant asked. "What's the deal with this place. Wendy City, Sue Dinosaur, Tommy Gun. Everything has a name. I wish there was something named 'Grant something'."

"There is! There is!" Lee told him excitedly. "There is a place here in Chicago called Grant Park. It has a really cool fountain. We have been there for school picnics before."

"Mommmm!" Grant yelled towards the front seat. "Can we go to Grant Park tonight? Pleasssse!"

His mother laughed and replied, "Not tonight dear. It's dark out there, and you can't go to a park in the middle of the night. Besides it will be bedtime when we get home."

"Awwww shucks, we never get to do anything fun," Grant muttered, as he sunk back down in the back seat. "I'm not six years old anymore, you know."

Mobster
Madness

No Grant
Park Tonight

That night the kids all gathered in the room where Christina and Grant were staying in Uncle Michael and Aunt Cassidy's house. They had somehow convinced their parents to let Lee and Lana spend the night, too.

Christina made everyone sit down and then pulled her cell phone out and held it in front of the boys.

"We have a new clue. I need your help to solve it."

"Ooooh, a clue!" Grant shouted. He hopped up and started jumping on the bed in excitement.

Christina pressed the button and the numbers appeared on the screen for all to see:

687386

A Clue In Code

What Does It Mean?

"What kind of clue is that?" Lee asked her. "How can anyone make sense of it? That's just numbers and we don't know the key to use to decode it."

"I don't know, but we'd better figure it out," Christina said. "Uncle Michael is depending on us. He meant *something* when he sent it. We just have to figure it out."

Christina was quite disappointed that Lee didn't know what it meant. They had finally gotten the clue they wanted, and now they were at a dead end.

"Let's ask my Dad tomorrow," Lana said. "He believes your uncle is innocent, so I know he will want to help us find him. But for now, I'm going to bed. My head hurts trying to figure out all this code stuff."

"Goodnight, sis. Goodnight, Christina. Goodnight, Greasy," Lee said with a chuckle.

"Goodnight, Look Out!" Grant laughed back at him.

Christina cracked a smile for the first time all night and said, "Goodnight, silly boys." Then she said quietly and seriously under her breath, "Goodnight, Uncle Michael."

What Does It Mean?

Goodnight!

12 SECRETS REVEALED

The smell of bacon and sausage drifted up to the room where the kids were asleep. Grant popped open one eye, and the sunlight shining through the gap in the curtains blinded him. It seemed early. He could sleep for another three hours, he guessed. He rolled over away from the bright sunlight and was just about to close his eyes again and drift back to sleep when he noticed how quiet and empty the room seemed. He sat up quickly and looked around through squinted eyes. He was the only kid left in the room—everyone else was gone!

Grant quickly shuffled down the hall, down the stairs, and toward the loud noises he heard coming from the kitchen. As soon as he turned the corner he saw what all the commotion was about. His Mom, Aunt Cassidy, and Mimi were all standing in the kitchen sipping on their cups

Good Morning!

Breakfast!

of coffee, while Dad was clanking the breakfast dishes together as he washed them in the sink. Papa sat at the table in his slippers reading the newspaper, while the other three kids were sitting closely together across the table, each eating a homemade biscuit.

"Hey, sport!" Papa said to him. "It's about time you got up, sleepyhead. You almost missed breakfast. Your mother saved you a plate. Go ask Mimi to get it for you and come back here and eat."

Grant quickly retrieved the plate of food and slid his chair down to the other end of the table right next to where Lee was sitting. "What's going on? You three sure got up early!"

Christina filled Grant in with the details. "We're trying to get someone to take us to the Field Museum so we can search for clues. But so far, no one will take us."

"My Dad will be here in an hour, so hopefully he will take us." Lana flashed a big grin and added, "I'll just give him my sweetest smile, and he'll do anything I ask."

After breakfast, the kids got dressed in the hopes that they would be taking a trip to the Field Museum of Natural History. Finally, after an hour of waiting, Lee and Lana's father, Marcus, arrived. Behind him were two other men.

Breakfast

To The
Museum?

Marcus led the two men into the kitchen where all the adults were gathered and the kids followed a few steps behind.

"Good morning, Marcus," Papa said to him as he entered.

"Good morning to you. Hope you all had a good night's sleep. Let me introduce you to Simon Donatello and Paulie Tollorio," Marcus said, pointing in turn to the two men as he spoke their names.

Christina took a moment to look the men over carefully. Simon was extremely well dressed. He wore a sharp black suit and his shiny, black shoes were polished so well that Christina could see Grant's reflection in them. His dark hair was brushed neatly in place, and he wore a pair of dark sunglasses, even while he was standing here inside the house.

The other man, the one called Paulie, was the exact opposite. He was quite big, but his clothes seemed almost a size too small. The bottom of his right pant leg had caught on the top of his sock and was sticking up. His black trenchcoat was quite wrinkled, and Christina noticed that he had left faint black footprints across the kitchen floor. Aunt Cassidy would not like that!

Marcus continued his conversation. "Simon is our

To The Museum?

Who's That Guy?

third partner that I mentioned. He was born and raised right here in Chicago. His family is well connected in the shipping industry out on Lake Michigan. They give a lot of money to the museums and historic preservation groups in the city. And, as I mentioned last night, it is his funding that allowed your Uncle Michael and I to find Louis and dig him up and bring him to the Field Museum."

"Yes, except that my precious dinosaur never arrived," Simon blurted, as he removed his sunglasses and placed them carefully in his jacket pocket. "I just want you to know, Cassidy, that I don't blame your husband. I believe people are innocent until proven guilty. However, the evidence against him does NOT look good. Has he contacted you? Have you heard anything from him?"

"No," Aunt Cassidy told him crossly. "I have heard nothing and no matter what evidence there is showing that my husband stole these dinosaurs, I know that he did NOT do it."

"Of course, ma'am, forgive me," Simon told her, with a slight bow. "As a matter of fact, my associate, Paulie, is an investigator and is trying to locate the dinosaurs and clear your husband's name."

During this conversation, Lana had been tugging on her father's sleeve. Finally he bent down and she

Who's That Guy?

Pssst! Psst!

whispered in his ear. "I have to tell you something!"

She pulled him into the next room where she nodded to Christina and said, "Go ahead, tell him."

Christina took a deep breath and began. "I've been getting messages from my Uncle Michael. They're here on my cell phone. Look! First he sent me a message that said 911. I knew that meant he needed help. Then he sent me these numbers: 687386. We haven't been able to figure out what the clue means. Lana and Lee thought you could help us."

"Kids!" Marcus Coyle exclaimed. "We *have* to give this information to the police. Simon and I are heading to the station this morning before we go to the museum. Let me have your phone and I will show them the messages."

Christina clutched the phone tightly and put it behind her back. "No, we *can't* tell the police; they want to arrest my uncle. Please don't tell *anyone*. We just wanted you to help solve the clue."

"Well, I don't have any idea what those numbers mean, but if they really came from Uncle Michael, then the police have to know," Marcus told her gently.

Lana knew Christina was upset, so she butted in and told her Dad, "Fine, but let Christina keep the phone and we'll tell you as soon as another message comes in."

Pssst! Psst!

A Michael Message

"Ok, girls. Let me know as soon as you get one. I have to go. The police officers are expecting us in less than half an hour. Come give your Dad a kiss goodbye, Lana," Marcus said, as he reached out and wrapped his arms around Lana, giving her a big hug.

Five minutes later, Marcus, Simon, and Paulie left together for the police station. While the four kids ran upstairs to change out of their pajamas, the adults made plans for the day.

From downstairs, came Papa's deep, bellowing voice, "Let's go kids, everybody load up the car with a smile–we're off to the Magnificent Mile!"

A Michael
Message

To The
Magnificent
Mile!

13 CAUGHT IN THE ACT

The door burst open and the rat-faced man barged in. He grabbed Uncle Michael by his shirt collar and pushed him up against the wall.

"So, you're sending secret messages to those meddlesome kids? Where is the thing you're sending these messages with? Just make things easy on yourself and hand it over."

Uncle Michael reached into his pocket and pulled out the pager. He reluctantly handed it over to the angry man. "Don't mess with those kids. Leave them out of it."

The beady-eyed man let go of Uncle Michael to take the pager. "Oh don't you worry about them. I'm gonna send them running in the wrong direction all over Chicago, and they'll believe that all these clues

How Are You Messaging?

Hand It Over!

59

are coming from you!"

"Not with my pager you won't, mister. The batteries are dead. It doesn't even light up anymore," Uncle Michael responded.

The man punched all the buttons with no response, so he decided that the pager was indeed useless. He then bent down to look Uncle Michael square in the face and snarled, "Those kids were too dumb to even figure out the last message that you sent them. If you keep trying to interfere with our plans, then you and those kids will both regret it. You got it, buddy?"

"Yeah, I got it," Uncle Michael replied sullenly. "Just tell me one thing. Who's buying my dinosaur?"

"I'm not sure, but I know they are picking it up in two days, and it's gonna make me a very rich man!" the rat-faced man responded gleefully, heading towards the door.

As he left the room he tossed the useless pager back over his shoulder towards Uncle Michael. "Arriverderci!" he said, slamming the door shut behind him.

Uncle Michael had grabbed the pager just before it hit the ground and leaned back against the

Hand It Over!

Arriverderci!

wall smiling in the dark. He chuckled to himself as he pulled the batteries out of his pocket and put them back into the pager. He hit the button and the screen light popped on. It was time to send another clue, he told himself.

Arriverderci!

Time for
Another Clue

14 New Clues – Magnificent!

"What is Magnet Mile?" Grant asked, as they drove down the road.

"It's Mag-nif-i-cent Mile, silly," Mimi told him. "It's one of the best shopping districts in the entire country. People come from hundreds and hundreds of miles away to visit the fancy shops here."

Oh great, Grant thought to himself. He hated shopping unless it was for toys, and he had a feeling that on this shopping trip that he would be dragged into a mile of girlie clothing stores.

Papa dropped them off in front of the store that Mimi pointed him towards. "I'll meet you inside in about ten minutes once I park the car," he told them.

Everyone else piled out onto the curb where all the girls immediately headed straight for the front door. Grant

The Magnificent
Mile Is . . .

Shopping?!?

looked at Lee. The boys shrugged their shoulders in defeat.

Lee took one last glance down the street. His eyes widened as he saw a huge yellow dinosaur with black polka dots down the side street a few blocks ahead. He rubbed his hands to his eyes and took another look. The street was empty. *I really have dinosaurs on my brain,* he thought to himself as he walked through the front door to the store.

Inside the store, Mom and Mimi 'ooohed' and 'ahhhed' over the fancy clothes on the racks. Christina and Lana tried to decide what they thought would make the best outfit for their dolls. Grant and Lee skulked around the store making loud, roaring dinosaur noises and giggling every time they startled someone.

"I'm a Shop-asaurus," Grant joked, as he sniffed through the racks of clothes, making his best hungry dinosaur grunts.

"I'm a Try-on-a-shirtus Rex!" Lee cracked back, grabbing a shirt off the rack and pretending to chew on it, slinging it from side to side.

Suddenly a hand reached out from the nearest clothes rack and grabbed Grant around the wrist. He spun around startled, and saw Christina and Lana peering out at him from the other side of the rack.

Shopping?!?

Come Here!

Looking around Chicago!

"Come here," Christina hissed at him. "We just got another clue!"

The four kids immediately gathered beneath the hiding place in the center of a rack of ladies dresses.

"What does it say?" Lee asked anxiously in a hushed tone. He was hoping that this clue would be easier to solve than the last.

"Look here," Christina said, holding up the cell phone for all of them to see the screen. The message read:

Take a ride to the top, where then it will stop. Another clue you will hear, if you head to the pier.

Each of the kids read the clue twice and all were quiet until Lee broke the silence saying, "We need to go to the Navy Pier! There's a big Ferris wheel out on the pier,

Come Here!

Another Clue!

and this clue must be telling us to ride the Ferris wheel!"

"Yeah, and then we will get another clue!" added Grant.

"Somehow we have to talk Mom into taking us to the pier," Christina told them. "If we all beg, then Papa will give in and take us!"

With a plan in mind, Grant scampered out from under the umbrella of dresses. He walked over to the bench at the front of the store where Papa was, sipping on his third cup of coffee.

"Papa," Grant said in his sweetest voice. "Will you please show me the Navy Pier and let us ride the big Ferris wheel? I'm *soooooo* tired of shopping."

Papa laughed and said, "That sounds like a great idea, sailor. Pack up your gear. We're off to the Navy Pier!"

Another Clue!

Off To The
Navy Pier

15 IN THE NAVY

Grant ran back to the other kids and told them the good news. They all immediately ran outside and waited on the curb for the adults to catch up. After another five minutes, Mimi, with armfuls of shopping bags, and Mom, with a wad of credit card receipts in her hand, finally came out of the store. They both unloaded their bags on Papa, who somehow managed to carry them all the way back to the car.

After a short ride in the car, during which the kids bubbled with excitement, the group arrived at the entrance to the pier. Christina looked out and asked with a bit of confusion, "Where are all the ships? How do the sailors work without any ships?"

Off To The
Navy Pier

Where Are
The Ships?

"The Navy doesn't use the pier, Christina," Mimi informed her. "It was named the Navy Pier in honor of the Navy personnel that served during World War I."

"It looks like a giant amusement park on a pier to me!" Grant exclaimed.

Lee grabbed Grant and Christina by the hands and shouted, "Come on!"

As they ran towards the big Ferris wheel, Lana shouted to them. "Wait, we've got to get tickets first!"

They ran straight to the ticket counter where Christina forked over the money for their tickets. While she was paying, she noticed a man in a dark trenchcoat and slouched hat sitting on a bench. He seemed to be staring right at her. With his hat pulled down over his eyes, she couldn't see his face, just his pointy nose sticking out. She felt a quick shiver, even in the bright sunlight, and tried to push the creepy man out of her thoughts.

As they ran to the Ferris wheel, Grant's short legs left him straggling at least ten feet behind the other kids. He shouted ahead, "I get to sit in the front!"

Lana shouted back, "There *is* no front seat on a Ferris wheel, silly boy! It just goes round and round."

"Whoa, I'm dizzy already!" Grant said, weaving back and forth as if he had just been spun in circles.

"You're a Dizzysaurus!" Lee joked, bellowing out his meanest dinosaur growl.

They reached the Ferris wheel and loaded up. Grant and Lee sat in one seat, the girls in the next. When the operator pushed the lever and the big wheel started turning, the kids all squealed in delight and began applauding. The Ferris wheel slowly gained speed until they were going round and round in circles high up into the sky.

"Maybe this is why they call Chicago the Windy City," Christina yelled, as she went round and round, her hair blowing in the wind.

Each time they reached the top, they would look out and try to wave to Mimi and Papa and Mom. But they were busy watching a man play a violin to a large crowd of bystanders. On the next pass over the top, Christina glanced down and saw the creepy man in the trenchcoat and hat standing at the bottom of the Ferris wheel, looking up at them. Her heart jumped as she watched the man walk over to the controls of the big wheel when the operator turned his back to talk to people waiting in line.

Christina grabbed Lana around the arm and squeezed hard in fear.

To The Ferris Wheel

Round And Round

"Ouch! Why did you do that?" Lana asked her, pulling her arm away.

"That . . . that man," Christina stammered. "I think he's going to do something to the Ferris wheel!"

Suddenly, just as their seat was at the top of the circle, they heard a loud screeching noise. The Ferris wheel jolted to a complete stop. Christina quickly looked back down and spotted the man running away from the Ferris wheel. She lost him when he disappeared into the crowds.

People came running from all directions to see what had happened. Papa was one of the first to reach the bottom of the ride. "What's wrong?!" he yelled at the operator.

Christina and Grant's mother waved up to them and shouted, trying to hide the worry in her voice, "Don't worry, they'll get you back down in a minute."

Up at the top, Lee and Grant were admiring the view. They weren't worried at all. However, in the next seat, Christina's concern grew as her phone buzzed meaning that there was another message.

She pulled out the phone as Lana looked on. She clicked on the display screen and there was the message:

Round And
Round

Stopped At
The Top

Christina was shocked. She knew that her Uncle Michael needed help, but now he was threatening them and telling them to give up. It just wasn't making sense.

"We've got to get down from here," Lana squeaked worriedly. "I don't like heights."

"Yeah, and we've got to figure out what's going on. Why did the clues change, and why is Uncle Michael telling us to stop looking for him?" Christina wondered.

An hour passed as they sat at what seemed the top of the world in the hot sun. The sweat dripped off their faces. Grant and Lee dreamed of good things to eat. Both were extremely hungry and wished that the firemen that had finally arrived would hurry up and get them down.

Stopped At
The Top

A Warning?

"I should have brought my bathing suit," Grant said to Lee. "No one told me that Chicago had an ocean!"

"That?" Lee asked him, pointing at the huge expanse of water at the end of the pier. "That's Lake Michigan. It's one of the Great Lakes. You can't even see from one side to the other it's so big. But it's not as big as the ocean."

"And no waves for boogie boarding like the ocean either," Grant told him.

Christina had been thinking about her latest message quietly for the last hour. She stared at Lake Michigan while she decided what to do next. She pulled out her phone again and punched in her return message:

IS THIS REALLY U
UNC MIC?

A Warning?

Waiting To
Get Down

Lana fidgeted in her seat. She did not like heights and hoped that someone would get them down soon. She looked out towards the city and tried to keep her mind off how high up they were.

Down one of the streets, near the front of the pier, she saw a huge orange and blue dinosaur with two large horns sticking out of the top of its head. Lana gasped and began to yell for Christina to look. But before she could get her first word out, she had blinked and the dinosaur was gone. She rubbed the sweat from her eyes and thought to herself, *I need to get down soon–I'm starting to go crazy!*

After another half hour, they finally got the Ferris wheel running again. The chairs finally circled to the ground where the passengers eagerly got off. Mom came running up and gave Christina and Grant the biggest hugs they had ever had.

The first words out of Grant and Lee's mouths were, "We're hungry!"

Even though her knees wobbled like Jello, Christina didn't realize she had been so worried. They trudged their way back to the car where Christina quietly told Grant and Lee about the new message that she had received. Neither could believe it! She also told them of the return question that she had sent.

Waiting To
Get Down

Finally Off
The Wheel

Christina decided to keep the man in the dark trenchcoat a secret for now. She had been though enough adventure on the Navy Pier for one day.

After a quick lunch of Chicago's famous deep dish pizza, they headed to their next destination. Mimi led them toward a ramp leading up to a long train. "We're going to ride the Loop!" Mimi informed them.

"Didn't we just ride the Loop?" Grant asked. "That Ferris wheel seemed pretty loopy to me."

"No, silly, the Loop is the nickname for the train system downtown," Mimi said.

"It's also called the 'L'," Lee volunteered. "For eLevated train. Lana and I have ridden the 'L' a bunch of times before."

"I'm getting dizzy again already!" Grant giggled, as he started walking in a zigzag stagger up the ramp.

Christina lagged behind, not speaking. She was worried about Uncle Michael.

finally Off
The Wheel

Lunch & To
The Loop

16 'L'LUSIONS

Mimi and Papa were taking them to a place called Printer's Row. Mimi explained to the kids that Chicago was full of book publishers. Today, on Printer's Row, all the publishers and bookstores would have stacks and stacks of books for sale.

Mimi, being a mystery writer herself, loved to browse through old bookshops for rare and interesting books. As a matter of fact, the whole family loved to read. After they boarded the train, the doors closed with a whoosh and it zoomed off down the tracks. The tall buildings whizzed by so fast that everything was a blur.

At one of the stops, Christina glanced through the open doors from her seat and looked directly at a man in a dark trenchcoat and grubby slouch hat walking toward the next car. She blinked her eyes quickly and he was gone. "I

The 'L' To Printer's Row

Off We Go!

must be seeing things," she mumbled to herself.

A few more stops later, the adults stood up and headed for the open doors. "Move out sailors," Papa announced to the kids. "Off we go to Printer's Row!"

They exited the 'L' with Grant and Lee doing their best dizzy impressions as they staggered and swooned down the ramp. Papa led them around a corner and right to the end of Printer's Row.

As far as Christina could see down the entire street, were tents filled with books, books, and more books. New books, old books, tiny little books with locks and keyholes on the front, and even some books at least two feet tall! She figured you must be able to find every book in the world here today. Mimi headed straight for a table stacked with some of the oldest looking books that Christina had ever seen.

They all slowly made their way down the street as a group. Papa's arms slowly got fuller and fuller as Mimi placed book after book in his hands for him to hold. It was obvious from the sweat on his forehead that they were starting to get quite heavy.

Grant and Lee hunkered over a table to browse through a book about dinosaurs. Lee was gave Grant a whole list of tidbits about the dinosaurs in the pictures they

Off We Go!

Books, Books, & More Books!

Off to Printer's Row!

were looking at. "That's the Brontosaurus. Sometimes he's called *Thunder Lizard* because he's so big it sounds like thunder when he walks. It's believed he had two brains–one in his head and one in his hip!"

"Wow!" Grant said, "He must have been the smartest dinosaur in the world."

"Not *too* smart, I bet!" Lee replied. "After all, there aren't any Thunder Lizards around anymore, so they couldn't have been students at the Jurassic Park School!"

Grant nodded his agreement and told him, "I can't wait to get to the Field Museum. I want to see Sue the T-Rex."

"Well, since the burglary, I'll bet she looks like a Tyrannosaurus Wreck now!" Lee joked.

Christina continued wandering down the long row of storefronts and tents stacked high with books. Lana stopped to look at a table that had a stack of Mimi's *Carole Marsh Mysteries* on it. As Christina reached an intersection in the street, she just happened to glance down the alley to the side. She stopped dead in her tracks at what she saw.

At least six blocks down the street, she saw the top of a huge dinosaur moving across the road. It was red with large yellow stripes and it quickly passed out of sight behind a building. She stared another few moments, but it

Books, Books, &
More Books!

Disappearing
Dino?

did not reappear. *I'm having hallucinations,* she thought to herself. *I've got to find Uncle Michael and the dinosaurs!*

Just as she was about to turn back and continue her walk through the maze of books, her throat tightened as she saw a familiar person down the alley. There he was—the same pointy-nosed man she had seen at the pier. He was hunched over looking at something in his hand. She stood there frozen, unable to move out of sight. Suddenly, he looked straight in her direction. He pressed the thing he was holding in his hand and placed it in his coat pocket. Slowly, he walked directly towards her.

Startled out of her frozen fear, Christina felt the buzz of her phone in her purse. She gave a last glance at the man in the black trenchcoat and turned and ran back up the street, straight to where Papa was still following Mimi around, now with an even taller stack of books in his arms.

Christina was breathing hard and sweat dotted her forehead. Her mother insisted that she sit down and rest on the bench next to where she was looking at books. Christina slumped down on the bench and peeked back down the street. The man was nowhere in sight. She secretly pulled out her cell phone and quickly checked the latest message:

Disappearing
Dino?

There He Is
Again!

Christina stood up on the bench and waved her hands in the air until she got the attention of Lee, Grant, and Lana. They all came running over and sat down on the bench next to her.

"Did you get another clue?" Lana asked her excitedly.

"Yes," Christina began, "but first I have to tell you about the man in the black coat. When we were at the Navy Pier, I saw a man in a dark hat and coat watching us. Then while we were on the Ferris wheel, I saw him go to the controls and stop the ride while we were up on top. Then I saw him again while we were riding the 'L'. Just now I saw

There He Is Again!

False Messages?

him down the alley, and I think *he* is the one that sent me this message!"

"You saw Uncle Michael running around in a hat and coat out here?" Grant asked her, puzzled.

"No, what's she's saying is that someone has been sending us false clues pretending to be your Uncle Michael, to keep us from figuring out where he and the dinosaurs are really hidden," Lee explained. "This clue is telling us to go to the Buckingham Fountain in Grant Park, I think."

"I've got a fountain in my park?" Grant chimed in.

"Yes, but we can't go, because the man in the dark coat might be there," Lana said determinedly.

Christina continued with her explanation. "I think the first clues we received were really from Uncle Michael. He was sending them in some kind of number code. Then after we told your Dad about the messages, we started getting the word riddles that are leading us in the wrong direction!"

"Wait a minute!" Lana squealed. "My Dad isn't the one who stole the dinosaurs! I know he would never try to hurt your uncle or us."

"Yeah, but we need to find out if he told someone about the messages. Maybe they are the ones who know where Sue, Louis, and Uncle Michael are," Lee said. "As

False Messages?

Secrets
Revealed

soon as we get back to the house, we can ask him."

The kids all nodded in agreement. Christina didn't want to believe that Marcus Coyle was the bad guy, but it just seemed like too much of a coincidence that they started receiving fake clues as soon as she told him about the messages.

"Let's go, boys and girls!" came Mimi's shout from across the street. The group of kids jumped up together and headed out of Printer's Row back towards the 'L' train.

Lee poked Grant in the side on the way up the ramp and said, "What's red on the outside and green on the inside?"

"I dunno know. What?" Grant asked.

"A dinosaur wearing pajamas!" Lee cracked a hearty laugh, as they all boarded the train and headed back home.

Secrets
Revealed

Back Home

17 A MESSAGE FROM MICHAEL

As the car pulled in the driveway, the kids were disappointed to realize that Marcus Coyle had not returned. Aunt Cassidy seemed happy to see them again as she poured each of the four kids a big glass of pink lemonade. She still looked weepy with worry though. "So how do you like Chicago?" she asked Grant and Christina.

"I don't understand this Wendy City," Grant began. "The 'L' train isn't shaped like an L, the Navy Pier has no Navy, and I didn't see anything magnificent on Magnificent Mile. And I haven't even gotten to see a single dinosaur yet!"

"We'll be going to the museum after dinner tonight," Cassidy informed the group. "I have to see the security guards at the museum to turn over the rest of your Uncle Michael's files. They are still hoping to find

Back Home

Museum - Tonight!

87

some clues as to what happened to him, Sue, and Louis. The curator, Clyde Baxter, has agreed to stay late to give you kids a special tour."

"Cool!" "Awesome!" "Great!" shouted the kids. All except Christina, who thought worriedly to herself, what if the man in the black coat is at the museum tonight?

The kids finished their drinks and headed upstairs. It wouldn't be long until they went to dinner, so they had to get ready. Lee and Lana's mom came to pick them up, leaving Grant and Christina upstairs alone.

"Do you think that Mr. Marcus is the bad guy?" Grant asked his sister.

"I hope not," Christina told him. "Lana and Lee believe that Uncle Michael is innocent, so I have to think that their father is, too. There *is* something about the man in the black coat that I can't put my finger on. I wish I had gotten a better look at his face. I just remember his long pointed nose."

"So we'll just keep an eye out for someone with a nose like Pinocchio carrying a dinosaur skull under his arm," Grant said, as he rolled on the floor laughing at himself.

"I'd rather see a dinosaur with a pointed nose

Museum -
Tonight!

Get Ready
for Dinner

carrying the bad guy under his arm!" Christina laughed back.

Once the adults were ready to leave, they piled into separate cars. Mimi, Papa, and Grant in one car; Mom, Dad, Aunt Cassidy, Cousin Avery and Christina in the other. Just as they were pulling out of the driveway Christina yelled, "STOP!"

"What's the matter?!" Dad asked.

"I forgot my phone. You told me to always carry it in case of emergencies," she replied.

Her mother turned around and told her, "Well, you probably won't need it, but run back inside and get it just in case. Better safe than sorry. Be sure to lock the door on the way back out."

The adults sat in the car talking while Christina ran in and grabbed the phone she had left upstairs. She was halfway back down the stairs when the phone suddenly started buzzing in her hands. She stopped at the front door and pressed the light to turn on the screen. She had gotten two messages! She checked the first one. It read:

This was her birth date! That means it must really be Uncle Michael sending this message. She quickly clicked down to the second message. It was another clue:

She had no idea what this could mean.

Christina shoved the phone into her pocket, closed and locked the front door behind her, ran back, and jumped in the car with Mimi, Papa, and Grant.

"You must have missed me!" Grant said, leaning his head against her as she sat down in the back seat.

"Sure, squirt," she responded, as she put her fingers to her lips to tell him to be quiet. She leaned over and whispered in his ear, "We just got another clue! And this one *really is* from Uncle Michael."

Grant's eyes widened and he held his breath as he waited for her to reveal the message to him. She just leaned back in the backseat and silently mouthed, "Wait until dinner."

Need The Cell
Phone!

Two
Messages!

Grant glared at her, crossed his arms, and slid to the other side of the backseat. If she doesn't want to share the clues, he thought, then he would just have to try to solve this mystery without her.

Once they reached the restaurant, Grant was excited to see that Lee, Lana, and their parents were already there. Christina rushed over to ask the kids if they had talked to their Dad.

"He said that he only told Simon and the police officer who was investigating the disappearance," Lee said.

"But he told us that Simon was with him all day, so that means that it can't be either one of them," Lana added.

Christina looked around carefully to be sure no one else could hear what she was about to say. "I got two more messages! I know that these are really from Uncle Michael."

She pulled out her phone and showed them the first message, explaining that it was her birth date, so that meant that Uncle Michael had to have been the one that sent that message. When she showed them the second one, none of them had any idea of what it might mean.

"110, 1454, and 120. What is he trying to tell us?"

Two Messages!

Really Uncle Michael

Lee wondered aloud.

"Maybe it's an address," Grant guessed. "1454 110th street in Room 120."

"Let's go ask!" Lana said, jumping up and running to tug on her Dad's arm. In less than a minute, she was back with a dejected look on her face. "He doesn't know, but if there is an address like that, it's a long way from here, he said." "We'll never get there tonight to check it out."

"I don't think that's it anyway," Christina told them. "Sorry, Grant. It was a good guess, but it just doesn't seem right to me. Keep thinking over dinner, maybe we can figure it out."

The kids were very quiet during the entire meal. Not one of them even cleaned their plate except Lee, who cleaned his, Lana's, and even part of Grant's plate. Grant, with his feelings still hurt from Christina's rejection of his idea, grabbed Lee's sleeve as they were walking out the door after dinner. He steered him towards Mimi and Papa's car.

"Ride with me," he told Lee. "I want to hear more about Tyrannosaurus Sue!"

Really Uncle
Michael

What Does It
Mean?

18 Your Number is Up!

The cars pulled out of the parking lot together. As Papa drove down the street, Mimi read a map and told Grant and Lee about the buildings they passed.

"That beautiful building on the right is the Civic Opera House. It was built all the way back in 1929. The two towers across the street are home to the 'Merc.' That's short for Chicago Mercantile Exchange. See that really tall building up ahead a few blocks? That's the Sears Tower! According to this map, the Sears Tower is 1,454 feet tall. That's 110 stories!"

Grant, who wasn't paying a lot of attention in the back seat, suddenly perked up. "What! Mimi, what did you just say?"

"That's the Sears Tower, the tallest building in the United States. It is 1,454 feet tall," she repeated.

What Does It Mean?

The Sears Tower

93

"And 110 stories!" Lee added enthusiastically.

Grant and Lee looked at each other with excitement. They had just solved one of the clues!

"Can we go to the top! Can we go, please!" Grant pleaded.

"Well, we are supposed to meet at the museum. However, it would be nice to see the city from the top at night," Papa remarked.

"Yes," Mimi agreed. "The rest of the group can wait on us. Besides, how often are we driving by the Sears Tower on a beautiful clear night like tonight?"

Papa pulled the car to a parking spot across the street from the building. Grant could hardly wait to get to the top. There must be a clue waiting. Papa paid for their tickets to get on the elevator, and they headed for the long trip up into the sky. When the elevator beeped and the doors opened, the four of them walked out onto the Observation Deck.

"Oh!" Mimi exclaimed. "Look how pretty the city is from up here. I've got to get some pictures! Maybe one day I'll write a mystery that takes place here in Chicago!"

The two kids searched the whole floor looking for some sort of clue. After they met back at the elevator, Grant shrugged his shoulders dejectedly. "I couldn't find a

The Sears
Tower

Up to The
Top

clue anywhere," he said.

"It has to be around here somewhere," Lee encouraged him. "The clue said 110. 1454. 120. We know that the 110 is the number of stories, the 1454 is the number of feet. What does the 120 stand for?"

The two boys walked slowly around the Observation Deck looking for anything that might have the number 120 on it. They found nothing. As Lee searched, he listened to the tour guide who was leading a group around pointing out different buildings. "The tall building to the northeast is the John Hancock Center. If you turn 90 degrees to the east, you will see Chicago's famous Navy Pier overlooking beautiful Lake Michigan. Continue turning to the south, and you will see Grant Park, the Art Institute of Chicago, and Buckingham Fountain."

"Excuse me, sir." Lee heard Grant's small voice ask the guide. "What would you see if you turned 120 degrees?"

"Let's see. . . 120 degrees," the guide replied to Grant as he turned and pointed. "If you look that way, you will see the Field Museum of Natural History, Adler Planetarium, and Shedd Aquarium."

"Thank you very much, sir!" Grant told him excitedly. Lee had heard every word and both of the boys

Up To The Top

Has To Be
The Museum!

could hardly contain themselves.

"It *has* to be the museum!" Lee exclaimed. "Your uncle and the dinosaurs have been there the whole time!"

"Let's get out of here," Grant said hurriedly. "Christina and Lana have a head start on us. We've got to solve this mystery first!"

Unfortunately, for the two boys, Mimi had another twenty minutes of pictures to make. Everything had to be just perfect for each shot. Grant almost couldn't stand it as he saw the hands on his Carole Marsh Mystery watch tick by slowly.

At the same time in the other car, Christina and Lana discussed their own ideas on decoding the clues.

"What if it's a phone number?" Lana suggested to Christina. "We could call and see if your Uncle Michael answers."

"Yea," Christina agreed. "That could be it! I'm only allowed to use my phone in case of an emergency though."

"This IS an emergency, an Uncle Michael emergency!" Lana told her and pointed at the phone.

"OK, here goes," Christina said worriedly. She

Has To Be The Museum!

Let's Go!

slowly dialed the numbers so that her mother wouldn't know she was using her phone. 110-145-4120. Christina held the phone close to her ear while she waited for someone to answer the other line. After three more rings she heard a voice on the line, "The number you have dialed has been disconnected or is no longer in service. Please hang up now."

"It's a wrong number," Christina informed her sadly. "It was a good guess, Lana."

"I just thought of it, because that sign back there said EXPERIENCE THE WINDY CITY. CALL 1-800-CHICAGO FOR DETAILS," Lana said.

Christina was confused. "How do you call CHICAGO on a phone?" she asked.

"Each letter matches up to a particular number on the phone. I'm always making up words with the phone numbers that I have to remember," Lana said proudly.

"Hmmm," Christina thought aloud. "Maybe that's the key to one of these clues from Uncle Michael." Christina checked her phone and listed the letters for each number in the clue for her and Lana: 687386. "Six=M,N,O. Eight=T,U,V. Seven=P,Q,R,S. Three=D,E,F. Another Eight and then another Six."

Lana quickly scribbled out the letters as Christina

Working On
The Clue

Letter Number
Connection

read them off.

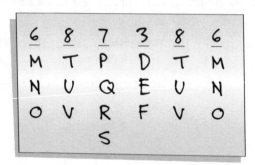

Both girls began sounding out words from the series of letters on the paper. "MUR . . ., OUR . . ., NUP . . .," Lana said aloud.

"NUS . . ., MUS . . .," Christina continued.

"MUSIC!" Lana cried, while doing a dance in her seat.

Christina checked the letters and realized that Lana was incorrect. "No, that doesn't fit. See, M U S, no I or C."

"Ohh, I C that there is no I or C," Lana joked, and both girls giggled.

"MUS . . . MUSEUM!" Christina suddenly shouted.

Christina's father thought that she was shouting at him. He shouted to the two girls over the seat, "We're

Letter Number
Connection

The Museum!

almost to the museum, girls. Hold your horses back there."

Christina double and triple-checked the letters. IT FIT!

"The museum! Your uncle and the dinosaurs must have been there the whole time!" Lana exclaimed.

"We've got to tell the boys as soon as we get there. We *have* to find Uncle Michael tonight!" Christina excitedly replied.

Time seemed to stand still as the girls waited for the car to reach the museum.

"On my way, Uncle Michael," Christina said quietly to herself. Then she sat back in her seat and sent one last message:

ON MY WAY.

The Museum!   On My Way!

19 CURIOUS CURATORS AND MYSTERIOUS MUSEUMS

The car pulled up in front of a building constructed of beautiful marble. Christina marveled at the enormous Greek columns in the front.

"You have something in common with this building Christina. This is the world's largest building made of Georgia marble," her father told her.

"But Dad, I'm not made of marble," Christina joked back in her best smart-aleck voice.

"Oh, really honey?" her father laughed. "I guess you're made of sugar and spice and everything nice?"

"Of course I am," she said sweetly. As soon as the car stopped, she and Lana bolted out of the backseat. They jumped on the curb and began looking for Papa's car with Lee and Grant in it.

"Where are they?" Lana asked impatiently.

The Museum!

Where Are They?

"Kids, let's go wait for everyone else inside," Aunt Cassidy said, as she headed up the long, wide flight of steps to the front door. Everyone followed her through the doors and into a huge atrium.

Christina was amazed at the size of the room. Her whole school would fit in this one room! The beautiful ceiling was dotted with skylights and the walls had prettier details than any she had ever seen before. Moonlight shone through the skylights and gave the atrium a creepy, tomblike feeling. Christina shivered as she noticed the long tusks of a big woolly mammoth up ahead.

"C'mon, there's the curator," Aunt Cassidy said, as she walked across the enormous room.

Christina watched as Aunt Cassidy approached the man. He was extremely tall and skinny and gave her a quick hug. The man had black hair and a small thin mustache across his top lip. There was something strange and creepy about the man. He also had two features that made Christina's heart drop. He was wearing a long black coat and had a long, pointed nose.

"Lana," Christina hissed, "I think that is the man in the black coat from the pier!"

"Really?" Lana asked, as she stopped in her tracks to eye the curator suspiciously. "How do we find out? Can

Where Are
They?

Is That The
Man?

we trick him into telling us where the dinosaurs and your Uncle Michael are?"

Christina and Lana wandered around the huge room while Aunt Cassidy handed over Uncle Michael's files to the curator. Christina's impatience grew as what seemed like at least twenty minutes had passed, and Mimi, Papa, and the boys had not yet arrived.

"I'll bet they stopped for ice cream," Lana suggested. "Lee thinks with his stomach first and his brain last!"

"Yea, he and Grant are both Pig-a-sauruses," Christina said, with a giggle.

Finally after another ten minutes, Christina heard Papa's booming voice echo throughout the hall. "Helllllo! Helllllo! Helllllo! Helllllo!"

Grant and Lee ran across the big room, skidding on the slick marble floor straight towards Christina and Lana.

"This place is awesome!" Grant said, between gasps for breath, as he slid to a halt next to the two girls.

"We solved the clue!" both Lee and Lana exclaimed to each other at the same time.

Christina nodded to Grant and told him of how they had decoded the first clue using the letters on the phone. As soon as she was done, Grant proudly went over every

There They Are!

We Solved The Clue!

detail of how they had figured out the Sears Tower clue.

Once they had congratulated each other on their brilliance, Christina pointed towards the curator and said, "I think that man is the one who has kidnapped Uncle Michael. He is wearing a black coat, has a pointed nose like the man at the pier, and he even has a key to the museum!"

"It *can't* be him," Lee interjected seriously.

"Why not?" Christina snapped.

"Because he's not wearing a big dinosaur skull around his neck!" Lee said laughing.

"This is no time for jokes," Christina replied sternly.

"Hey kids," came a call from across the room. Aunt Cassidy was waving her arms for the four of them to come over to where she was talking to the creepy-looking curator.

Hesitantly, they shuffled slowly over to where the two of them were standing. Each kid eyed the man warily and stopped ten feet before they reached where he stood staring at them.

"Yes?" Christina managed to stammer.

"This is Mr. Clyde," Aunt Cassidy began. "He is the curator of the Field Museum and is going to take you four on a personal tour."

"Hello, children," Clyde responded gruffly with a

We Solved The Clue!

A Special Tour

quick nod at the kids. "I have a special tour planned for the four of you," he finished, flashing them a crooked, evil grin.

"Ummm, mi-mi-mister?" Grant stuttered. "What's that hanging around your neck?"

The curator picked up the small item hanging on a leather thong around his neck and held it out for Grant to see. "This is the skull of a Mussaurus, one of the smallest dinosaurs, called *mouse lizard*. It's the first fossil I ever found when I used to dig up dinosaurs, just like your Uncle Michael."

With that said, he abruptly turned and walked off towards a dark hallway. Spinning around, he snapped, "Follow me, children. Your *special* tour is about to begin."

The four kids reached out and grabbed each other's hands. They all squeezed them tightly as they slowly followed the *creepy* curator into the darkness.

A Special Tour

Creepy
Curator

20 TOUR TERRORS

"The field museum originally opened in 1893," the curator informed them, as he led them down the dim passageway. "It was named the Field Museum in 1905, after Mr. Marshall Field, a major benefactor of the museum. In 1921 the museum was moved to its present location."

The curator led them through a large doorway, and they entered a room that reminded Christina of pictures she had seen of Africa. He stopped in front of two massive, stuffed lions. "These are the infamous Man-eaters of Tsavo," he said. "In 1898, these two monstrous beasts killed and ate over 140 men in East Africa!"

"Sounds like these two were the T-Rex of lions," Lee popped up and said.

"Just wait," the curator said slyly. "I've got a T-Rex

Creepy Curator

Man-eaters!

107

for you to see."

He continued his dizzying tour through a maze of rooms as they zigzagged their way through the displays. They marveled over exhibits of tuxedoed penguins, insects the size of dinner plates, unusual artifacts from Africa, Native American houses big enough to walk through, and so much more that Christina felt lost. She couldn't even remember where they began.

As they passed one particularly dark hallway, Christina spied a curious door, with a chain and padlock wrapped around the doorknob. "What's that door go to, Mr. Clyde?" she asked.

"That goes down to the basement of the museum. It's been closed for over 50 years, ever since they had a fire down there. I don't think anyone has been down there in eons. It's very dark and scary down there," he replied, giving her a sinister grin as he continued walking.

Christina gave Grant a poke in his ribs and pointed to the floor. Grant looked down and saw black footprints on the floor leading away from the door. "Looks like *someone* has been in there recently," he mumbled to her under his breath.

Mr. Clyde suddenly stopped outside of a large, arched doorway and turned to face them. The room behind

Man-eaters!

familiar
footprints

him was completely dark. "This is end of the tour for you kids. It's my favorite part," he said, an evil grin on his face. "Get ready for a real treat!"

He stepped into the darkness and disappeared. Suddenly the lights in the room burst on and they saw the gigantic skeleton of a headless dinosaur dominating the center of the room ahead.

Lee and Grant rushed in excitedly.

"It's Sue!" Lee yelped. "Actually, it's headless-Sue!"

"She's absolutely Sue-per!" Grant shouted.

"This is our most famous guest," Mr. Clyde bragged. "Sue went on permanent display here in May of 2000. She was the largest and most complete Tyrannosaurus fossil yet to be discovered at that time. Louis, the T-Rex that your Uncle Michael and Marcus discovered, is even more complete, but unfortunately, it now seems the museum may never get to display him."

Grant marveled at the amazing dinosaur skeleton towering above him. How incredible it would be to find one of these! One day he would become an 'Indiana Bones' paleontologist, just like his Uncle Michael!

"What do *you* think happened to Sue's head and Louis?" Christina asked the curator.

He answered her question in a low, secretive voice,

Familiar
footprints

It's Headless
Sue!

"If *I* were to steal a dinosaur, I would hide it so that I was the only one who would ever be able to see it. I would create my own personal private museum."

A moment later a squawking noise came out of the curator's pocket. He removed a walkie-talkie, pressed the button on the side, and said, "Clyde here."

Christina eavesdropped and heard the reply from the person on the other end, "It's time. You need to come back to the office now."

Curator Clyde returned the walkie-talkie to his pocket and said to the kids in an agitated voice, "I've got to go. Follow that hallway through those doors ahead to get back to the atrium when you are done in here." Without a second glance, he stormed out of the room and disappeared down the hallway.

They were left all alone. Well, *almost* all alone.

It's Headless
Sue!

Almost All
Alone

21 SUE-PER SECRET PASSAGEWAYS

The boys continued to gawk at the dinosaur in the center of the room.

"It's sooo cool!" Grant told Lee for the third time.

"Sue is the coolest 'She-Rex' in town," Lee joked back at him.

Christina wandered back into the hallway where they had come from. She knew they had to somehow get past the locked door into the basement, *if* she could remember how to get back there. She called out for Lana and the boys to follow her.

She quickly led them through the maze of pathways and exhibits. After they passed the same polar bear for the third time, Lee said, "I think we're lost."

"We're not lost," Christina snapped back. "I'm just not sure where we are."

Almost All Alone

Where's The Basement?

A noise up ahead caused the kids to duck behind the polar bear display. Christina peeked out from around the bear's head, while the other kids peeped between its legs. They saw a man in a dark coat and hat rush down the hallway from the direction they had just come.

"It's creepy Clyde," Lana squealed. "He's coming to get us!"

"Hurry!" Christina egged them on. "We have to get to the basement before he finds us."

"Follow me!" Lee shouted as he ran from the room through the same doorway that the man had just gone through. The other kids were close on his heels as they weaved their way down hallways and around sharp corners. Suddenly he came to a halt. "We're here," he told them smugly.

"Good job," replied Christina. "You wouldn't happen to have a key too, would you?" she asked, as she stared at the chain and padlock wrapped around the doorknob.

"*I've* got a key," Grant told them, as he dug though the many pockets of his dinosaur vest.

The three kids looked at him, puzzled, until he pulled out the huge shark's tooth that he had received from Uncle Michael. "Here is *my* key. Hit the lock with this and it will bust right open!" he said, handing the tooth to Lee.

Lee took the purse-sized tooth in both hands and struck the lock with the sharp end. The lock popped open on the first hit. He stepped back, grinned, and handed the tooth back to Grant.

"Good job, Musclesaurus," Lana teased, as she helped Christina pull the chain from around the lock.

"No problem!" he responded in his best Arnold Schwarzenegger voice, flexing his muscles.

They slowly opened the creaky door and peered inside. The darkness ahead seemed imposing and scary. Grant removed a small flashlight from his vest. "It's a good thing I came prepared," he said proudly.

"Yeah, you're doing such a good job, Grant. Why don't you lead?" Christina told him, as she pointed to the thick darkness ahead.

Grant turned his flashlight towards the dark and noticed a steep set of stairs leading down. He slowly crept through the door and headed down into the basement. The others followed closely. As they reached the bottom of the stairs, the light from above disappeared behind them. Everything was dark except for the small beam of light from Grant's flashlight.

The floor cracked under their feet with each step. A burnt smell filled their nostrils. Grant led them gingerly

Locked!

Down Into The Dark

down the long hallway until they reached an intersection. "Left or right?" he asked.

"Right is always right," Lana suggested. Grant made the turn to the right and continued his slow trek forward with the rest of the crew close on his heels. After only a few feet, the passage stopped at a wall.

"Dead end!" Grant informed them.

They heard a rustling from above and felt a rush of air as something swooped past them. Grant spun around quickly and caught the culprits in his light. "Bats," he said. "Using their sonar to cruise for girls."

The girls ducked and squealed.

"Shine the light up there," Christina insisted, pointing to something she thought she had seen on the wall.

Grant aimed the light's beam at the spot and illuminated a rope hanging from the wall above.

Without a second thought, Lee reached up and gave the rope a swift tug. A foot-long piece of wood clattered to the floor. Moonlight shone through the small window that was revealed.

Christina slowly squinted at the ceiling above. She realized that something seemed to be moving. "What are those?" she asked timidly.

"Bats!" Grant whispered back. "Hundreds of them!"

Down Into
The Dark

What Are
Those?

Down into the dark basement!

"Don't disturb them," Lee instructed them all. "They won't bother you if you don't bother them."

"Yikes!" shrieked Lana loudly, when she felt something land on her head. She wiped something from her hair and held her hand out into the light.

"Yuck, it's guano," Christina told her.

"What's that?" Lana asked.

"Bat poop!" Lee laughed.

Lana screamed loudly and swatted at her hair with her hands. The loud noise caused a stir up above. Suddenly the passage was full as the startled bats flapped their wings and filled the air around the children.

"Ruuunnn!" yelled Christina.

In unison, the four kids turned and sprinted away from the swarm of bats. They ran past the turn where they had decided to go right before and kept running though the darkness. After more steps they realized that the bats were gone and they were safe.

"Right is definitely, NOT right!" Lee told his sister.

"Yucky bat poop," Lana grumbled.

Grant directed his flashlight ahead down the passageway and they realized they were in front of a large charred metal door.

Christina stepped forward and turned the handle.

What Are
Those?

Bats!

The heavy door creaked loudly as it slowly slid open. Grant pointed his small flashlight into the room. All they saw was darkness. Cautiously, they crept though the doorway. As they entered the room, the beam from the flashlight lit up glimpses of objects standing up around them.

"Hey, I found a light switch," Lee said as he flicked it up filling the chamber with blinding light.

Grant's eyes squinted shut from the shock of going from darkness to light. After a few seconds to adjust, his eyes began to refocus. Directly in front of him only a foot above his head, was an enormous gaping mouth lined with rows of sharp teeth.

"Agghhh! Don't eat me!" Grant screamed, tumbling backwards into Christina and Lana and causing everyone to fall to the floor in a pile like dominoes.

Quickly their eyes adjusted as they looked around the room. The walls were stacked high with bones, skulls, fossils, and animal skins. Directly in the center of the room was the one that had scared Grant half to death. It was a partially assembled T-Rex skeleton with a huge skull hanging just above their heads.

"That's Louis!" Christina guessed excitedly.

"And Sue's skull!" Lana added.

"This must be where the curator is keeping his own

Bats!

Louis & Sue's Head!

secret museum. He must have been the one who stole them," Lee said.

"We have to tell the police now," Grant said to his sister. "So they can find Uncle Michael."

From the entrance to the room came a voice the kids knew they had heard before.

"Well, well, well, Paulie, whatta we got here?" Simon said.

"Looks like four meddlesome kids to me, sir." Paulie replied.

Startled, Christina stepped back startled when she saw Paulie. He was dressed in a black trenchcoat and his pointy nose stuck out from under his low slung hat. He had a menacing look on his face as he stared at the kids.

"Looks like they found our little hiding place, eh. No problem, just makes it easier to get rid of them," Simon said to Paulie smugly.

"Be my pleasure, boss," Paulie replied, clenching his fists and smiling at Lee, who returned his evil grin with a wild-eyed stare.

"Let them see their Uncle Michael for one last time first. We might as well get rid of all of them at the same time," Simon instructed.

Paulie headed towards a door partially hidden behind

Louis & Sue's Head!

Uh Oh!

a huge lion skin hung on the wall. He jerked the door open and disappeared into the dark room. Moments later he emerged dragging Uncle Michael under his arms.

"Uncle Michael!" Grant exclaimed.

Uncle Michael lifted his head and gave the kids a small smile.

"Nice job kids. You solved the clues and found me. I'm sorry to get you in this mess with me."

"Don't worry, Uncle Michael, we'll get out of this–*somehow*," Christina told him in her bravest voice.

Paulie glared at them meanly and said, "You aren't going anywhere, heh heh!" He slowly approached the kids, then reached out and grabbed Lee by the arm. The kids scattered backward, except Lee who was trapped in the rat-faced man's clutches.

The two of them struggled directly under the towering skeleton of the missing T-Rex. Grant reached out and yanked the closest leg bone with all his might. With his second tug, the leg broke free and hurled him back onto the floor. The remaining bones of the skeleton came crashing down in a pile on top of Lee and Paulie. The monstrous skull landed on Paulie's head with a loud thud. He collapsed to the floor unconscious.

Lee's head popped out of the pile of bones and he

Uft Oft!

Pile Of
Bones!

hurried back to where the rest of the kids stood. Simon bent down and picked up a large femur bone that had shattered in half during the collapse. He pointed the splintered end directly at Grant.

"I think I'll start with you, you little pest," he said. He kicked his way through the pile of bones as he advanced towards Grant, swinging the bone like a bat.

Grant stood frozen in fear. Simon closed to within only a few feet of where he stood. He raised the large leg bone above his head and got ready to strike.

"Freeze!" came a shout from behind Simon. Through the doorway rushed a mob of security guards followed by the curator. The guards surrounded Simon and he dropped his weapon and raised his hands in the air. He hung his head in defeat.

Curator Clyde walked over to Uncle Michael and extended his hand and pulled him to his feet. "It's great to see you again!" he exclaimed. "And you kids, too!

"Plus my beautiful Sue and Louis!" he finished, as he looked over at the large skull and piles of bones on the floor.

While the security guards took Simon and Paulie away in handcuffs, Uncle Michael asked, "How did you know we were down here?"

"Sir, we got a call from the police that a little girl had

Pile Of Bones!

freeze!

called 911 and claimed there were robbers and kidnappers in the basement of the Field Museum," he replied.

Uncle Michael turned and looked over at Christina. "I wonder who that little girl was?" he asked with a big smile.

"*This* was definitely an emergency," she said, as she held up her phone. Uncle Michael laughed and nodded his head in agreement.

"We've got to get these fossils upstairs for display," Clyde said to Uncle Michael urgently.

"It can wait till tomorrow, Clyde. Tonight I'm going home to relax with my family and my little rescuers," Uncle Michael told him, as he gave a quick wink to both Grant and Christina.

As the group headed out of the room to go back upstairs and out of the basement, Grant took one last long look at the pile of bones scattered on the floor. "Now *that* is what I call a Tyrannosaurus Wreck!" he joked.

"Yeah, it's been a real dino-mite adventure!" Lee kidded back.

freeze!

Tyrannosaurus Wreck!

22 PRO BONE-O

Mimi, Papa, and the rest of the adults were all ecstatic to see them as they appeared from the dark entrance to the basement. There were many hugs to go around. Uncle Michael wrapped his arms around Aunt Cassidy and the baby and squeezed them tight.

Christina began telling the adults about the events that had happened since they left on their museum tour. "I even got to finally use my phone!" Christina said excitedly. "And this time is was really an emergency!"

"Bats? Skulls? Villains?" Mimi asked. "This sounds like quite a mystery adventure. I might have to write a story about all this one day."

"Put me in it, please," Lana told her.

"And me too!" Lee added.

"If you want to get really weird, Mimi, you can even

Look - It's Uncle Michael!

Colorful Dinos

talk about multi-colored dinosaurs roaming the streets of Chicago," Christina said.

"Hey," Lee shouted. "How did you know I imagined I saw a huge yellow dinosaur walking the streets?"

"I thought I was hallucinating when I saw an orange and blue dinosaur go by while we were stuck on top of the Ferris wheel," Lana told the group. "I was going to say something, but by the time I blinked, it was gone."

"I saw a red one with yellow stripes near Printer's Row," Christina said. "I thought I must be too stressed about solving this mystery. I thought if I told you about what I saw, you would think I had really gone crazy!"

"You guys are *all* nuts," Grant told them. "Big colorful dinos walking the streets of the city? You must think I'm five years old if you think I'll fall for that one."

"Actually, your friends are correct," Curator Clyde told them, as they approached the main lobby. "Follow me. I have one last treat for you children."

They hesitantly followed him again after a little assurance from their Uncle Michael. He led them out the front door of the Field Museum, down the long row of steps, and around the side of the beautiful building. The rest of the adults followed along behind the kids.

When the four kids turned around the corner of

Colorful Dinos

One Last Treat

the building, their eyes gazed upon the most unique sight they had ever seen. Row after row of crazy-colored dinosaurs lined the grassy field before them. Red ones, polka-dotted ones, tie-dyed ones, and rainbow-colored ones. Short ones and tall ones. Tall necks, long tails, big horns, and sharp teeth. There was every variety of dinosaur that they could imagine!

"What are all of these?" Grant asked in awe.

Clyde said, "These are for the museum's dinosaur celebration this weekend. People all over the city have been making their own crazy colored dinosaurs for a parade and have been bringing them here for the last few days. See that purple one with the pink swirls? That one is mine. I have been decorating it every night for the last week. Thanks to you kids, Sue will be back in one piece for all her admirers to see and the celebration will be bigger than ever!"

"I'm going to be sure you kids are the Grand Marshals of the parade!" Uncle Michael said. "After all, you saved the day. The museum got Sue's head back, you found out who stole Louis, and you saved me!"

"All in a day's work, Uncle Michael," Christina said, as she hugged him again.

One Last Treat

Dino
Celebration!

"I can't wait to be in a parade," Grant told him. "I want to ride on the biggest T-Rex there is!"

"I can't wait to see you. I *dino* what I would have done if I had missed it," Uncle Michael said and laughed. "But right now, I want to act like a Meatosaurus and EAT, EAT, EAT!"

The End

Dino Celebration!

Meatosaurus!

Grrrrrrr! Playing dinos!

A BOUT THE AUTHOR

Carole Marsh is an author and publisher who has written many works of fiction and non-fiction for young readers. She travels throughout the United States and around the world to research her books. In 1979 Carole Marsh was named Communicator of the Year for her corporate communications work with major national and international corporations.

Marsh is the founder and CEO of Gallopade International, established in 1979. Today, Gallopade International is widely recognized as a leading source of educational materials for every state and many countries. Marsh and Gallopade were recipients of the 2002 Teachers' Choice Award. Marsh has written more than 25 Carole Marsh Mysteries™. Years ago, her children, Michele and Michael, were the original characters in her mystery books. Today, they continue the Carole Marsh Books tradition by working at Gallopade. By adding grandchildren Grant and Christina as new mystery characters, she has continued the tradition for a third generation.

Ms. Marsh welcomes correspondence from her readers. You can e-mail her at carole@gallopade.com, visit the carolemarshmysteries.com website, or write to her in care of Gallopade International, P.O. Box 2779, Peachtree City, Georgia, 30269 USA.

Built-In Book Club
Talk About It!

1. Who was your favorite character? Why?

2. What did you think happened to Uncle Michael when his truck was found near the Field Museum, but he and the dinosaur bone were missing?

3. What was your favorite part of the book? Why?

4. You learn a lot about Chicago by reading this book. If you visited there, what would you like to see and do?

5. There are a lot of clues in this mystery. Which ones did you think were hard to figure out, and which ones were easy?

6. What was the scariest part of the book? Why?

7. Did you think that Clyde the Curator was the bad guy? Why or why not?

8. What do you like most about reading mysteries?

Built-In Book Club
Bring It To Life!

1. Make a list! Divide the book club into two teams. Ask each team to make a list of all the things they can remember about Chicago. That includes food, places to go, sports teams, museums, things to do—just everything that comes to mind! The team with the longest list is the winner!

2. Build a city! Construct a three-dimensional Chicago using miniature objects, cardboard, toothpicks, cotton ball clouds, grass, etc. You could even make an edible version and eat it during your book club meeting!

3. Express Yourself! Uncle Michael and his wife have special license plates that say "Mr. Bones" and "Mrs. Bones" because he loves dinosaurs so much. Ask each book club member to design a personal license plate and present it to the group.

4. Have a pizza party! Chicago is well known for lots of great food, including deep-dish pizza. Ask for a parent volunteer to bake a deep-dish pizza, or order one from a local restaurant. Brainstorm about why everyone loves pizza so much, and why you can find such a variety of ethnic food in Chicago.

DYNAMITE DINO

The tooth of a Tyrannosaurus Rex was 6-8 inches long.

The Dinosaur National Monument quarry is located near Vernal, Utah.

The Brontosaurus was also known as "Thunder Lizard."

Dinosaurs lived during the Mesozoic Period.

The Stegosaurus was bigger than an elephant, but his brain was the size of a walnut.

Dinosaur Canyon is located in Arizona.

SAUR TRIVIA!

The Braichosaurus' nostrils were on top of his head.

The Ptersaur was also called "hairy devil."

Deinosuchus were giant crocodiles that measured 48 feet in length.

The Brontosaurus was thought to have 2 brains: one in its head and one in its hip.

Dinosaurs swallowed stones to grind up their food.

Tanystropheus had a 21-foot long neck.

CHICAGO

Places To Go & Things To Know!

Field Museum of Natural History – building (world's largest made of Georgia marble) features dinosaur skeletons, stuffed elephants, and a pharaoh's tomb

Berghoff – the oldest functioning restaurant in the city, originally built for the 1893 World's Fair in Chicago

Magnificent Mile – features the best shopping in Chicago, some say in the best in America; includes several high-end designers and department stores

Navy Pier, – once part of a former naval training center, now the entertainment strip down the 3,000-foot pier includes a Ferris wheel, fountain, musical stage, even palm trees

Grant Park – features the Petrillo Music Shell for summer concerts and music festivals, the Richard J. Daley Bicentennial Plaza (ice skating in winter and roller skating in summer), the Buckingham Fountain, and two sculptures

Buckingham Fountain, in Grant Park, Chicago, Illinois – pink Georgia marble fountain offers a digitally-coordinated show of water and colored lights each summer

Printer's Row, Chicago, Illinois – spot along the South Loop that features a book fair which takes place each June

The "L" Loop, Chicago Transit Authority – elevated public train that winds through Chicago, also connected with historical sectors of the city – Loop Tour Train trips with Chicago Architecture Foundation tour guides available on Saturdays

The Civic Opera House – built in 1929, has housed the Lyric Opera of Chicago since the 1950s

The Chicago Mercantile Exchange – twin towers, where stock trading takes place, known as "The Merc"

Sears Tower – world's second tallest building, 110 stories, 1,450 feet high, features two observation decks for panoramic views

John Hancock Center, Chicago, Illinois – built in 1970 on Michigan Avenue, structure measures 845 feet in height

Art Institutes of Chicago – museum includes priceless works by artists Seurat, Van Gogh, Toulouse-Lautrec, Cezanne, Renoir, Monet, and Gauguin

Adler Planetarium – features collection of antique astronomical instruments, domes projection theater, Sundial sculpture, and star-gazing rooms

Shedd Aquarium – world's largest indoor aquarium

GLOSSARY

conspiracy: plotting secretly to do something illegal

culprit: a person accused or guilty of a crime

dejectedly: downcast, discouraged, and depressed

dire: dismal, distasterous, or desperately urgent

emphatically: to express in a firm and forceful manner

gallivant: to travel or roam wherever one likes

gawk: to gape or stare at stupidly

gingerly: in a cautious and careful manner

hunker: to crouch or squat

meddlesome: to act unrestrained or rudely; to be actively interested and/or involved in someone else's business

menacing: to act in a threatening manner, endanger

sinister: the appearance of evil in something or someone

swoon: to droop, faint, or fade

warily: to show caution and logical discipline, especially in noticing, confronting, and escaping danger

SCAVENGER HUNT!

Recipe for fun: Read the book, take a tour, find the items on this list and check them off! (Hint: Look high and low!!) *Teachers: you have permission to reproduce this form for your students.*

__1. Sears Tower

__2. a dinosaur bone

__3. Navy Pier

__4. weinerschnitzel

__5. Magnificent Mile

__6. bats

__7. 'L' train

__8. a mastadon

__9. Ferris wheel

__10. Printer's Row

WRITE YOUR OWN MYSTERY!

Make up a dramatic title!

You can pick four real kid characters!

Select a real place for the story's setting!

Try writing your first draft!

Edit your first draft!

Read your final draft aloud!

You can add art, photos or illustrations!

Share your book with others and send me a copy!

Six Secret Writing tips from Carole Marsh!

Non-fiction is factual!

1. Make up good titles – wild and crazy is good!

2. Use strong verbs – action verbs with pizzazz!

3. Edit your work to make it better!

4. Use your own special "voice" to make your work unique!

5. Use a thesaurus and dictionary to find the words that mean what you want to say!

Fiction is made up!

6. Don't worry about rules – use your imagination and have fun!

WOULD YOU MYSTERIES LIKE TO BE
A CHARACTER IN A CAROLE MARSH MYSTERY?

If you would like to star in a Carole Marsh Mystery, fill out the form below and write a 25-word paragraph about why you think you would make a good character! Once you're done, ask your mom or dad to send this page to:

> Carole Marsh Mysteries Fan Club
> Gallopade International
> P.O. Box 2779
> Peachtree City, GA 30269

My name is: _____

I am a: _____ boy _____ girl   Age: _____

I live at: _____

City: _____ State: _____ Zip code: _____

My e-mail address: _____

My phone number is: _____

_____

_____

_____

_____

_____

_____

_____

Enjoy this exciting excerpt from

THE WHITE HOUSE CHRISTMAS MYSTERY

1 'TIS THE SEASON TO BE ... BORED?

Christina stared through the big bay window in her grandmother Mimi's living room. She sighed, watching the rain that pelted the scraggly bushes and dull brown grass. What a dreary December day! Her younger brother Grant contentedly played with his Matchbox cars under Mimi's glorious gold and white Christmas tree. He could amuse himself anywhere, Christina thought jealously. She was tired of reading, tired of playing, and most of all, tired of school!

"Why don't we call your friends April and D.C. and ask them to come visit for a while?" asked Papa, Christina and Grant's grandfather.

"OMKHAY!" exclaimed Grant, whose mouth was full of gingerbread cookie.

Papa went to call April and D.C.'s mother while Christina stared at the sparkling white lights on the Christmas tree. They reminded her of stars in the winter sky. She made a wish on one of them . . . for something exciting to happen.

"Hello!" shouted April as she dashed through the front door. She dragged D.C. by the hand behind her.

"Boy, is it ever wet out there," said D.C. "I don't see why we get rain instead of having snow like everyone else in the country." The big story in the news was the blizzard that was blanketing much of the nation in snow.

As D.C. finished speaking, the phone rang, and Christina ran to answer it. "Hello?" she said.

A stern, very official-sounding voice asked for her grandmother. "It's for you, Mimi," she said, handing her the phone. Christina wondered whom the stern voice belonged to and why they were calling Mimi. She went and sat down at the big white kitchen table where Grant, April, D.C., and Papa were starting a card game of Go Fish.

Mimi rushed into the kitchen with a huge grin on her face. "It's final!" she exclaimed.

"What's final?" Christina and Grant asked at the same time.

"Our private tour of the White House!" exclaimed Mimi. She continued, "I'm planning to write a book about the White House, and Papa and I planned a tour so I could do some research. We thought it would be a fun Christmas surprise for us to take you and Grant along. You can each bring a friend along to Washington, D.C."

Christina and Grant looked at April and D.C. "You want to come, don't you?" Christina asked.

"D.C. is going to D.C.," sang Grant.

"You silly!" said Christina. "By the way, what does D.C. stand for?" she asked.

"It stands for Denise Claire," explained D.C. "I was born in Washington D.C., so my parents gave me a nickname that matched the place were I was born."

"D.C. also stands for the District of Columbia, the name chosen for America's capital city. The land for the city was taken from the states of Maryland and Virginia," Christina said in her *I know everything* voice.

Grant didn't respond by poking fun at his sister's typical know-it-all sort of statement. He looked crestfallen. "But what about school?" he asked downheartedly. "Christmas vacation doesn't start for another week."

"Your Mom and I have already settled it with the school," said Mimi. "The principal approved your absences because your trip will be an educational one."

"IPPHHHEE!" shouted Grant, who was eating gingerbread again. He even had crumbs in his head full of white-blond ringlets.

"We leave in four days, so start packing your bags!" said Papa.

Christina didn't hear him because she was daydreaming about the trip. Her wish for something exciting had come true! Only she hoped that the trip wouldn't be TOO exciting. Every time she and Grant went on a trip with Mimi, they ended up getting sucked into a real-life mystery. She hoped this trip would be in the Christmas spirit and not involve any other types of spirits . . . or ghosts . . . or missing people–especially not anyone like–say–Santa Claus!

THE CAROLE MARSH MYSTERIES SERIES

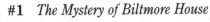

Visit the Carole Marsh Mysteries Website

www.carolemarshmysteries.com

- *Check out what's coming up next! Are we coming to your area with our next book release? Maybe you can have your book signed by the author!*

- *Join the Carole Marsh Mysteries Fan Club!*

- *Apply for the chance to be a character in an upcoming Carole Marsh Mystery!*

- *Learn how to write your own mystery!*